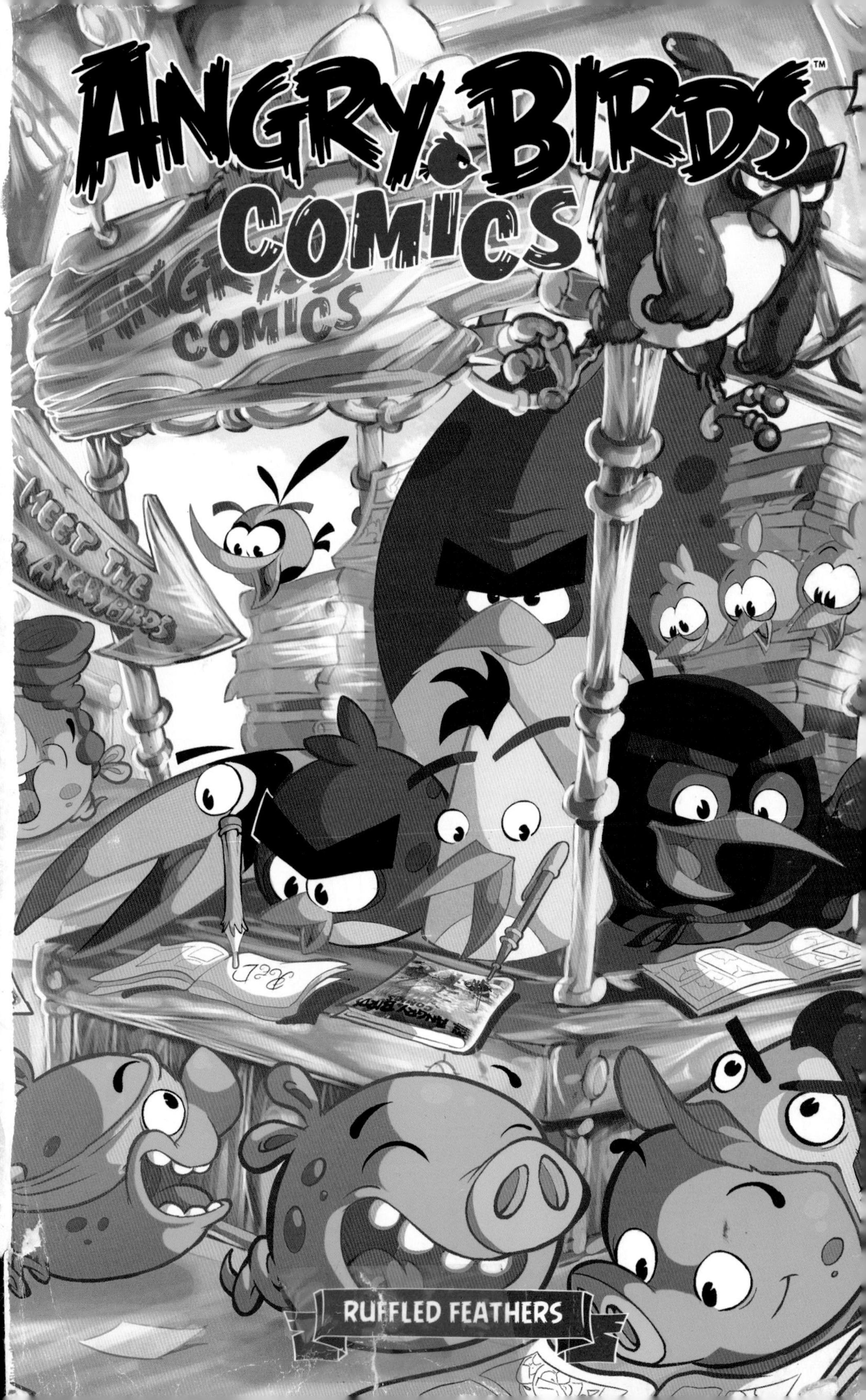

ANGRY BIRDS
COMICS
ANGRY BIRDS COMICS
MEET THE ANGRYBIRDS
RUFFLED FEATHERS

COVER ARTWORK BY: MARCO GERVASIO
COVER COLORS BY: NICOLA PASQUETTO

EDITED FOR IDW BY: DAVID HEDGECOCK
COLLECTION EDITS BY: JUSTIN EISINGER & ALONZO SIMON
COLLECTION PRODUCTION BY: CHRIS MOWRY
PUBLISHER: TED ADAMS

KAIKEN
PUBLISHING LTD.

Mikael Hed, Chairman of the Board
Laura Nevanlinna, Publishing Director
Jukka Heiskanen, Editor-in-Chief, Comics
Juha Mäkinen, Editor, Comics
Jan Schulte-Tigges, Art Director, Comics
Henri Sarimo, Graphic Designer
Nathan Cosby, Freelance Editor

ROVIO

Thanks to Jukka Heiskanen, Juha Mäkinen, and the Kaiken team for their hard work and invaluable assistance.

ISBN: 978-1-63140-762-8

19 18 17 16   1·2 3 4

www.IDWPUBLISHING.com

Ted Adams, CEO & Publisher
Greg Goldstein, President & COO
Robbie Robbins, EVP/Sr. Graphic Artist
Chris Ryall, Chief Creative Officer/Editor-in-Chief
Matthew Ruzicka, CPA, Chief Financial Officer
Dirk Wood, VP of Marketing
Lorelei Bunjes, VP of Digital Services
Jeff Webber, VP of Licensing, Digital and Subsidiary Rights
Jerry Bennington, VP of New Product Development

Facebook: facebook.com/idwpublishing
Twitter: @idwpublishing
YouTube: youtube.com/idwpublishing
Tumblr: tumblr.idwpublishing.com
Instagram: instagram.com/idwpublishing

ANGRY BIRDS
SUN DANCE
WE'RE CHIRPIN' IN THE SUN...
HOORAY!
BRAVO!
AB 2014-004
...JUST CHIRPIN' IN THE...
IT LOOKS LIKE YOU HAVE TO PERFORM YOUR 'SUN DANCE' SOME OTHER TIME.
SECOND TRY:
WHAT A GLORIOUS DAY...
EIGHTH TRY:
...I'M HAPPY AGAIN...
MAYBE YOU SHOULD COME UP WITH SOMETHING ELSE.

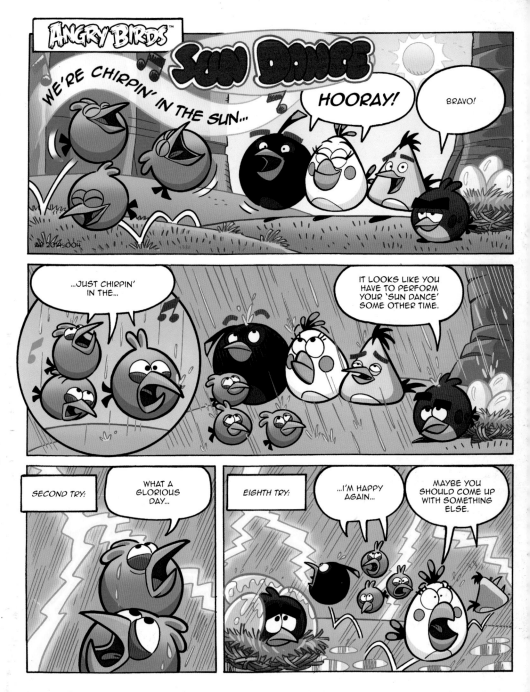

WRITTEN BY: JANNE TORISEVA • ART BY: MARCO GERVASIO • COLORS BY: DIGIKORE WITH B. DESHMUKH • LETTERS BY: PISARA OY

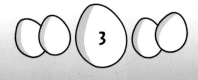

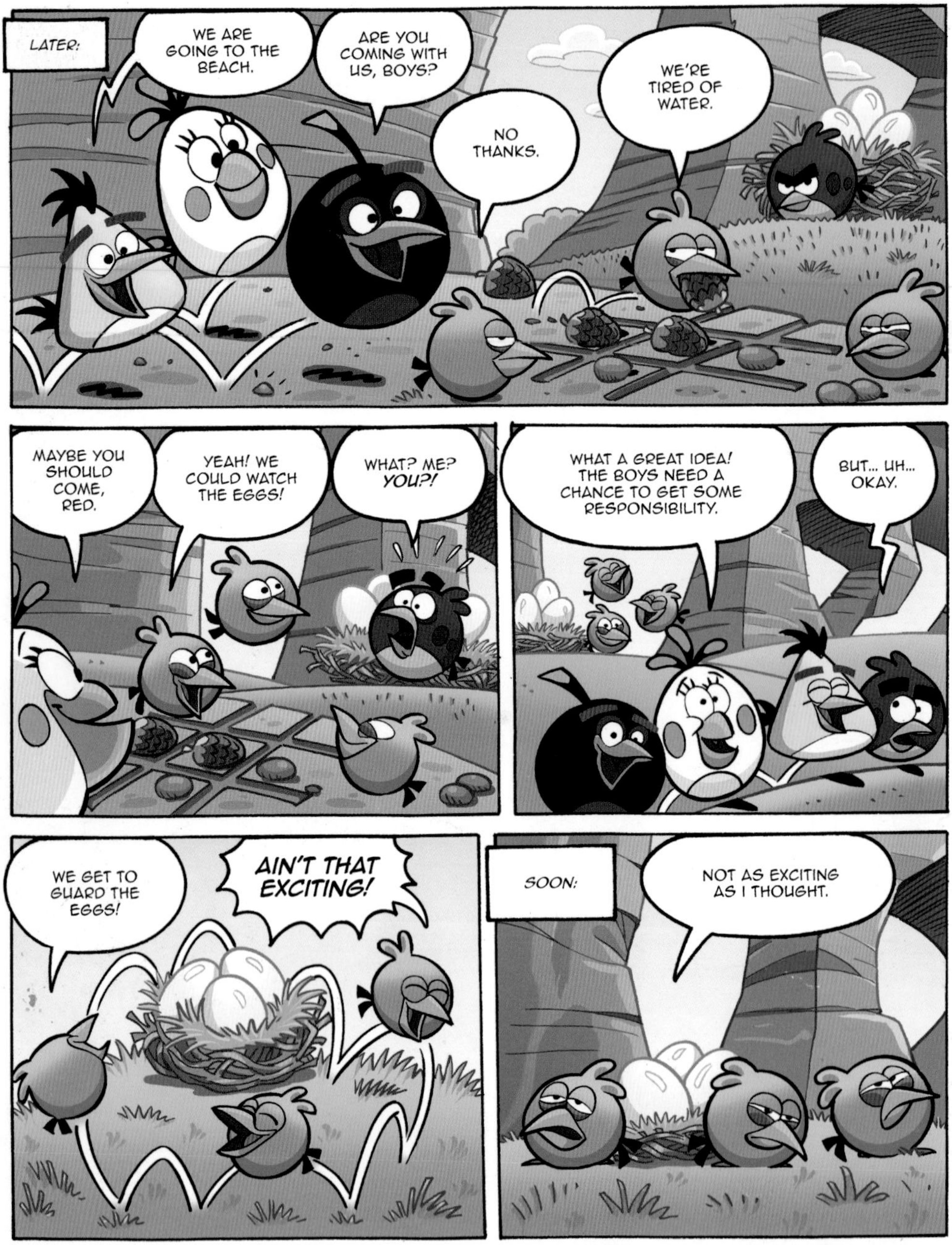
LATER:
WE ARE GOING TO THE BEACH.
ARE YOU COMING WITH US, BOYS?
NO THANKS.
WE'RE TIRED OF WATER.
MAYBE YOU SHOULD COME, RED.
YEAH! WE COULD WATCH THE EGGS!
WHAT? ME? *YOU?!*
WHAT A GREAT IDEA! THE BOYS NEED A CHANCE TO GET SOME RESPONSIBILITY.
BUT... UH... OKAY.
WE GET TO GUARD THE EGGS!
AIN'T THAT EXCITING!
SOON:
NOT AS EXCITING AS I THOUGHT.

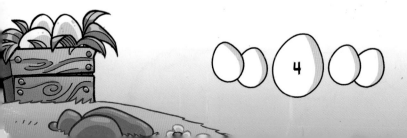

MAYBE WE SHOULD PRACTICE OUR 'SUN DANCE' AGAIN.
YEAH. AT LEAST IT WOULDN'T HARM ANYONE ELSE NOW.
GOOD MORNING SUNSHINE!
THE BIRDS SAY HELLO!
WOOOO
!
WOOOSH

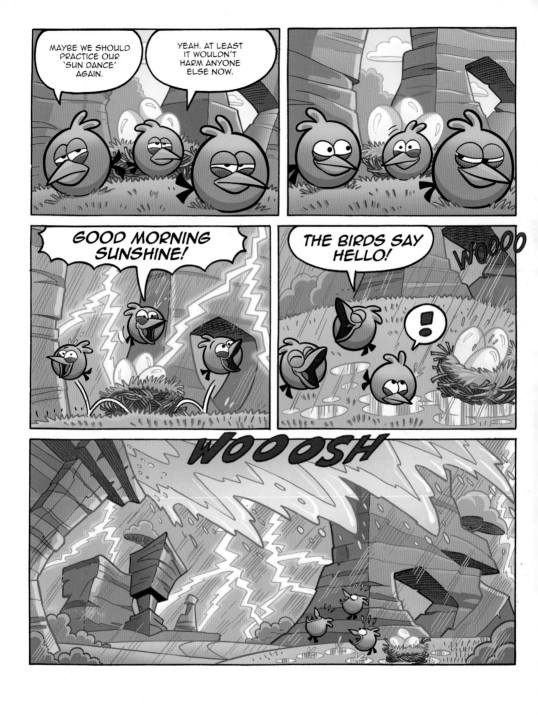

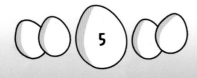

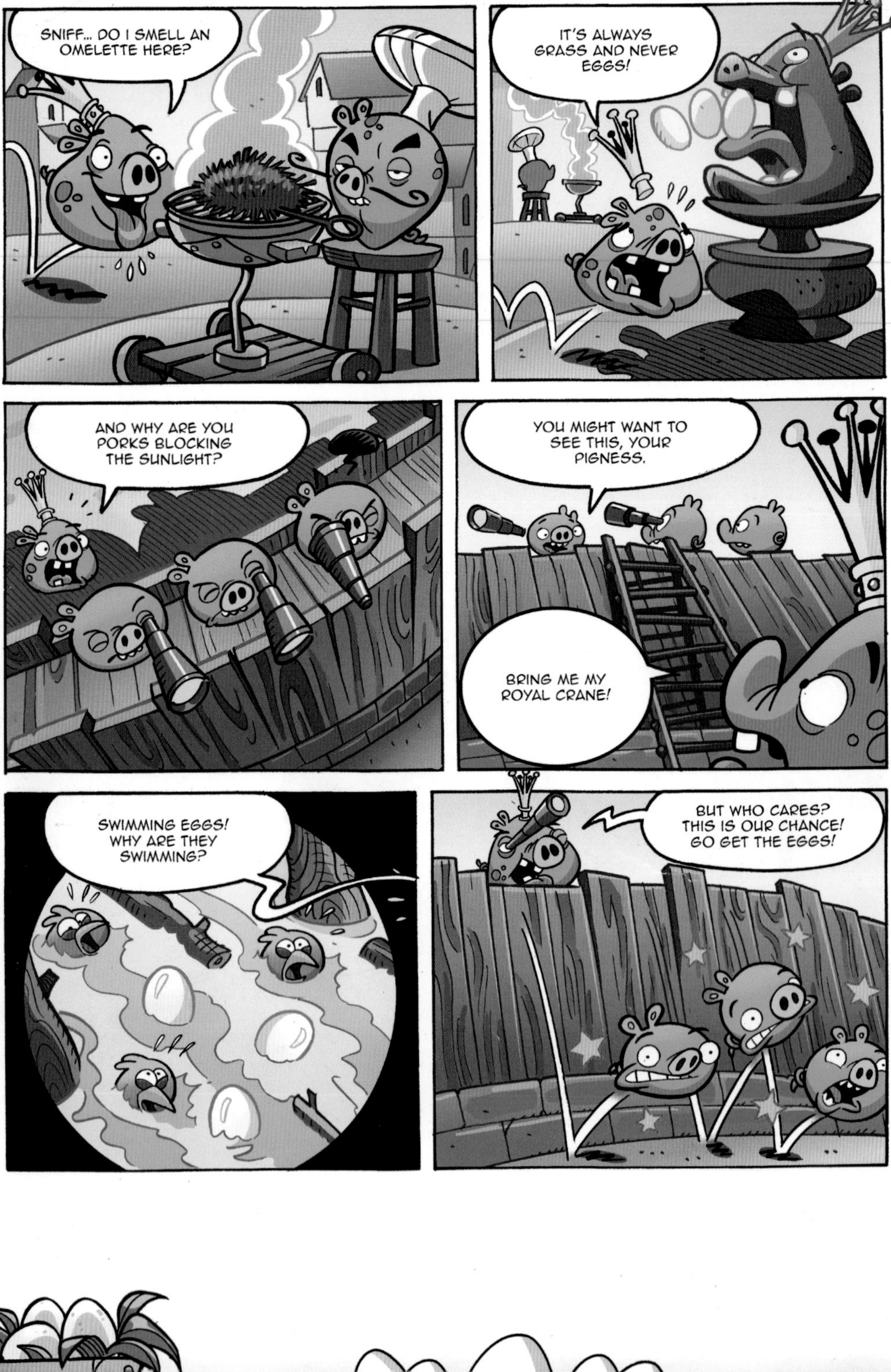
SNIFF... DO I SMELL AN OMELETTE HERE?
IT'S ALWAYS GRASS AND NEVER EGGS!
AND WHY ARE YOU PORKS BLOCKING THE SUNLIGHT?
YOU MIGHT WANT TO SEE THIS, YOUR PIGNESS.
BRING ME MY ROYAL CRANE!
SWIMMING EGGS! WHY ARE THEY SWIMMING?
BUT WHO CARES? THIS IS OUR CHANCE! GO GET THE EGGS!

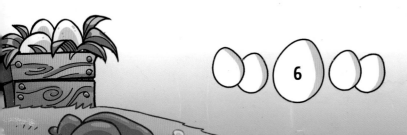

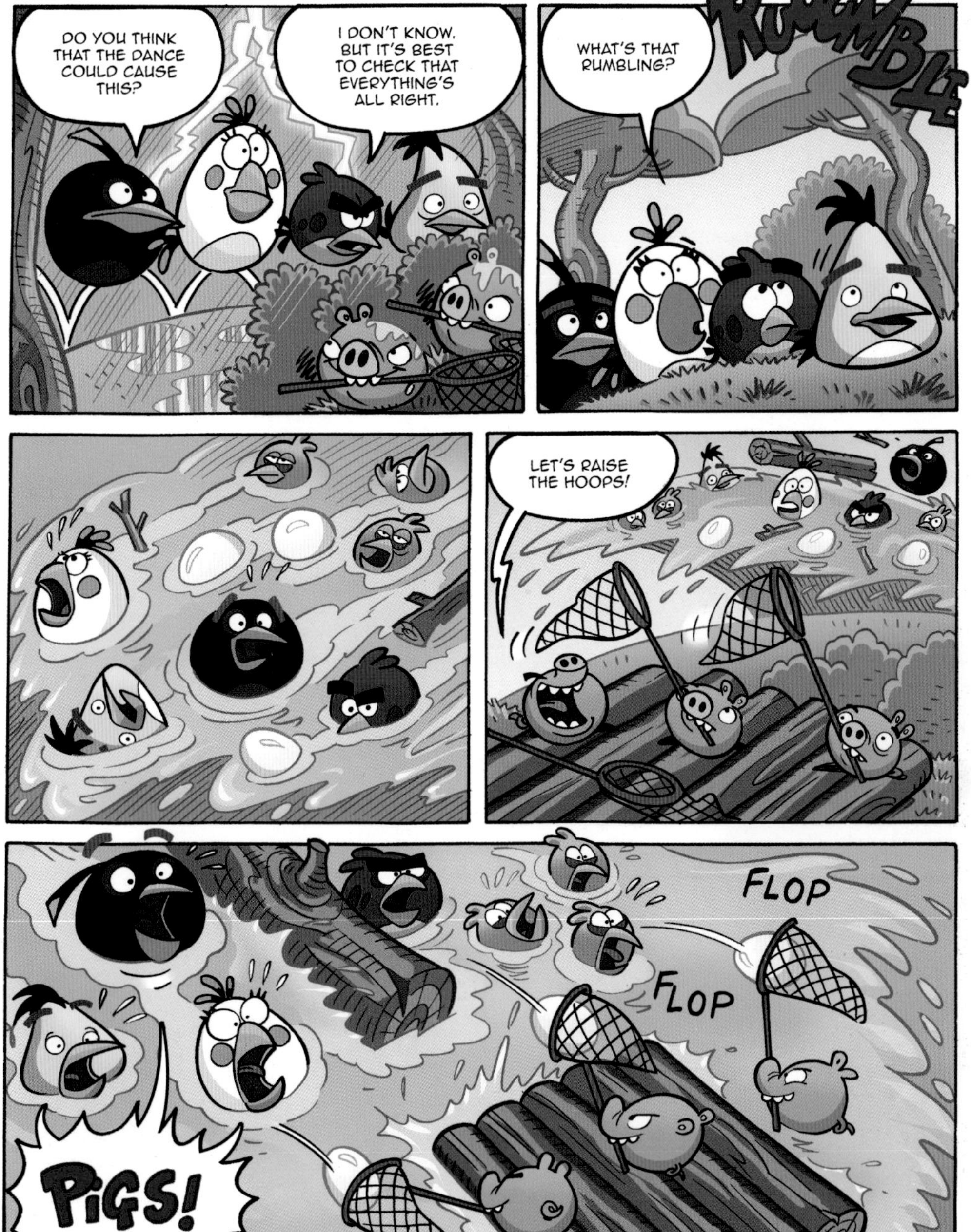
DO YOU THINK THAT THE DANCE COULD CAUSE THIS?
I DON'T KNOW. BUT IT'S BEST TO CHECK THAT EVERYTHING'S ALL RIGHT.
WHAT'S THAT RUMBLING?
RUMMMBLE
LET'S RAISE THE HOOPS!
FLOP
FLOP
PIGS!

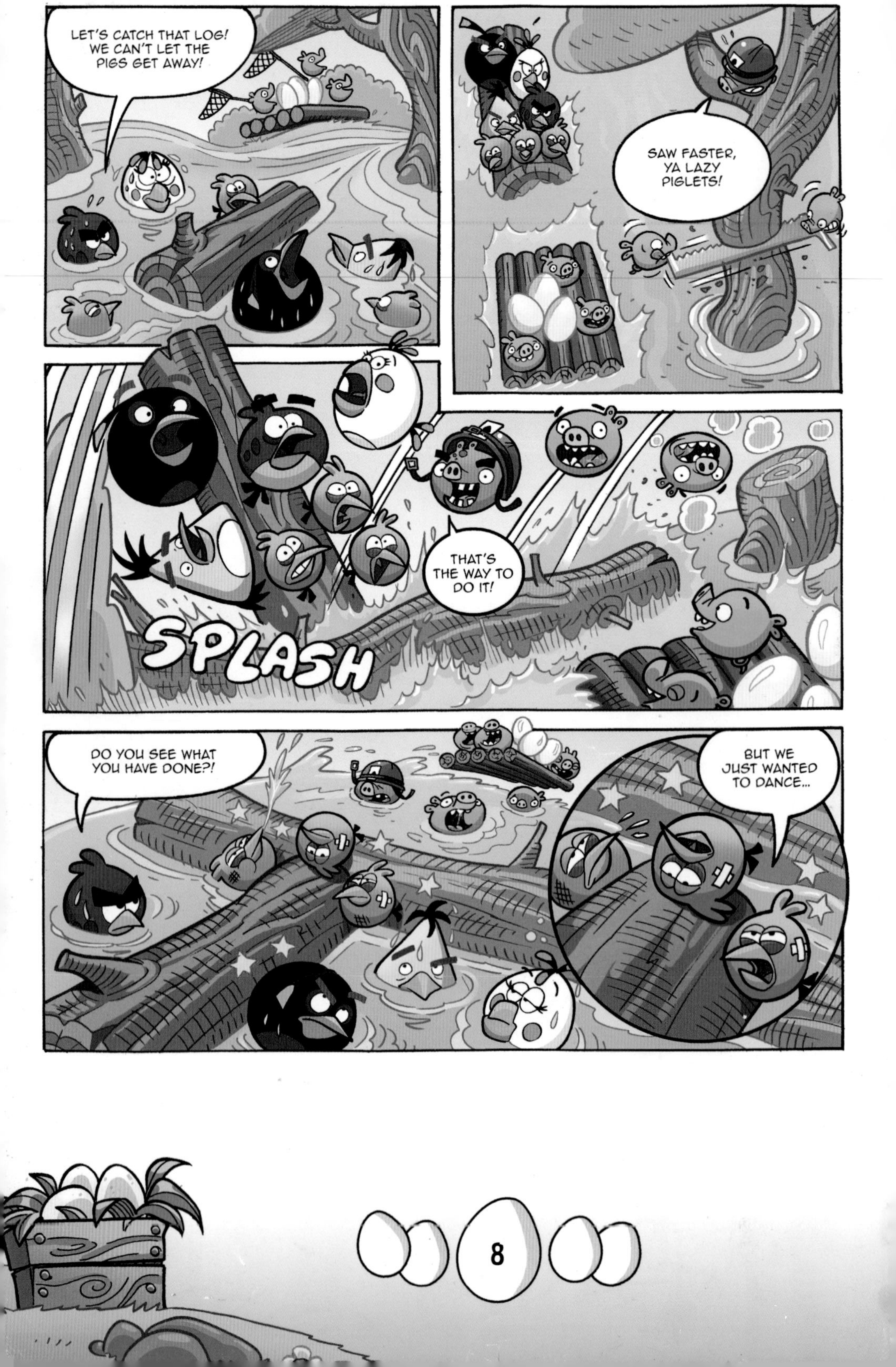
LET'S CATCH THAT LOG! WE CAN'T LET THE PIGS GET AWAY!
SAW FASTER, YA LAZY PIGLETS!
THAT'S THE WAY TO DO IT!
SPLASH
DO YOU SEE WHAT YOU HAVE DONE?!
BUT WE JUST WANTED TO DANCE...

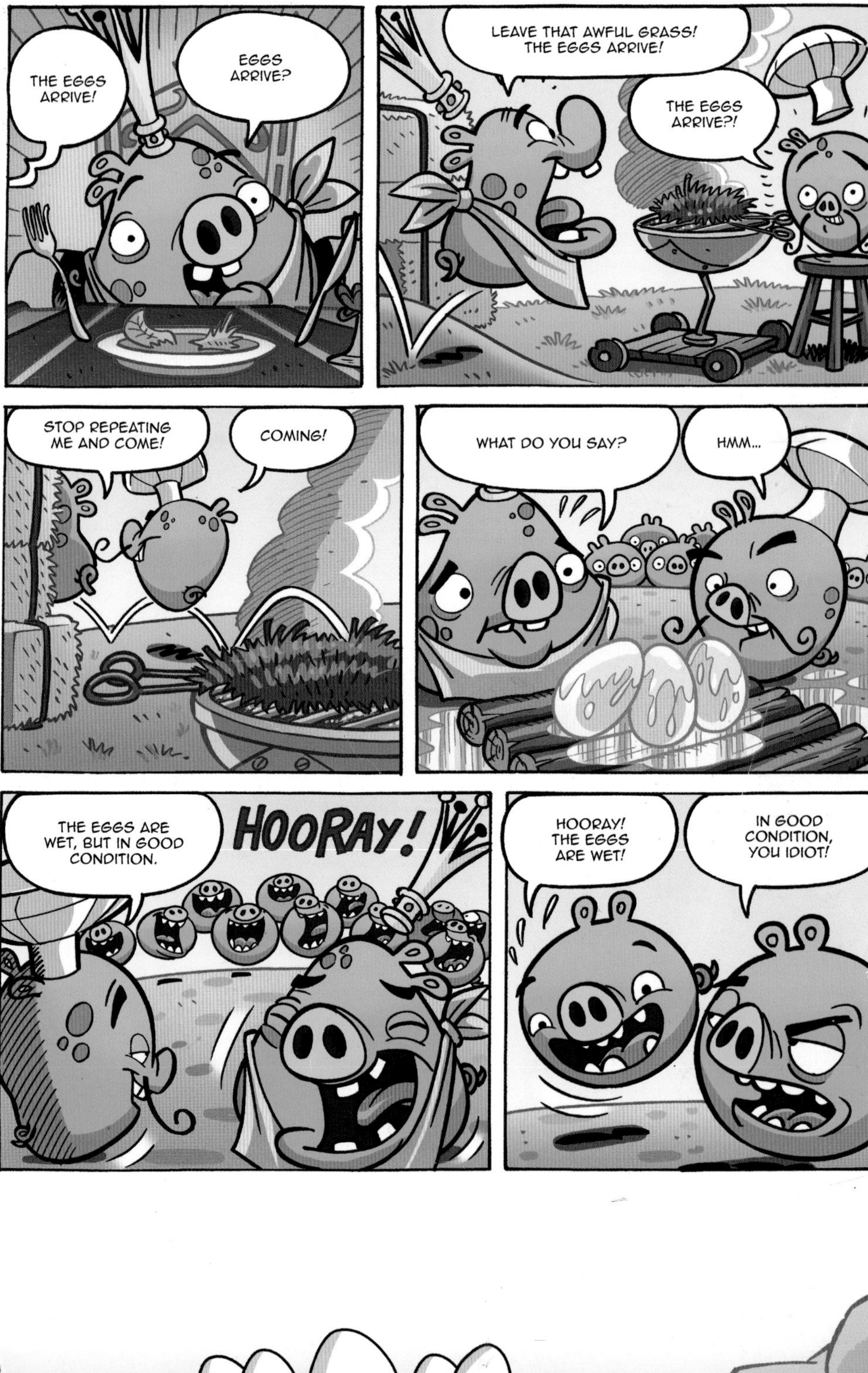
THE EGGS ARRIVE!
EGGS ARRIVE?
LEAVE THAT AWFUL GRASS! THE EGGS ARRIVE!
THE EGGS ARRIVE?!
STOP REPEATING ME AND COME!
COMING!
WHAT DO YOU SAY?
HMM...
THE EGGS ARE WET, BUT IN GOOD CONDITION.
HOORAY!
HOORAY! THE EGGS ARE WET!
IN GOOD CONDITION, YOU IDIOT!

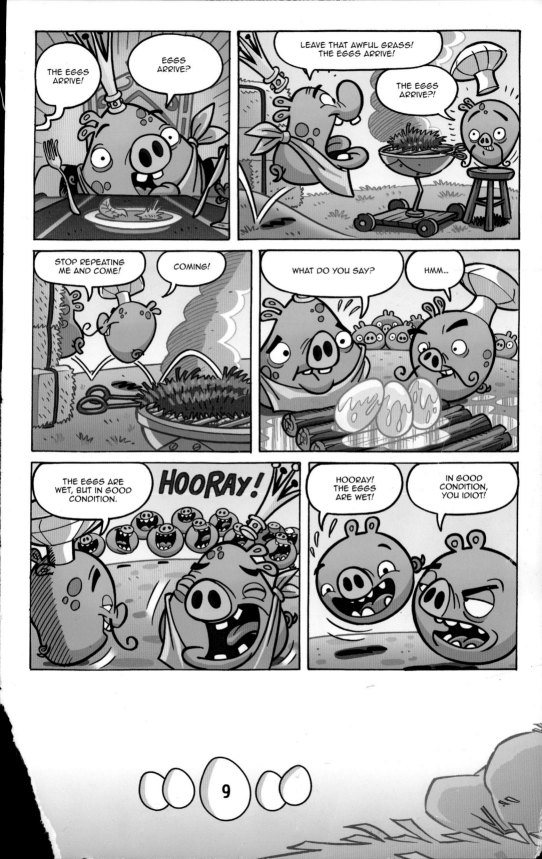

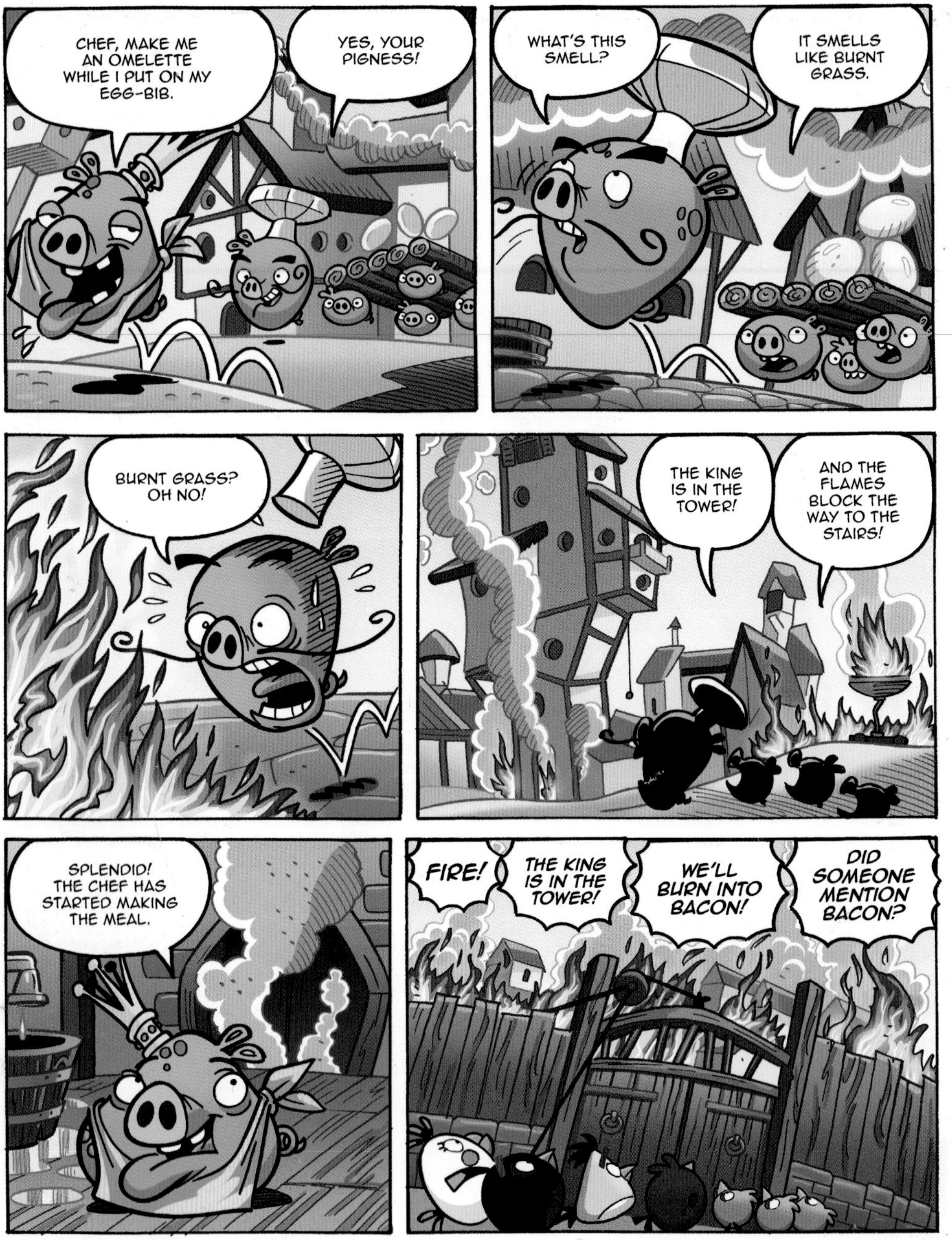
CHEF, MAKE ME AN OMELETTE WHILE I PUT ON MY EGG-BIB.
YES, YOUR PIGNESS!
WHAT'S THIS SMELL?
IT SMELLS LIKE BURNT GRASS.
BURNT GRASS? OH NO!
THE KING IS IN THE TOWER!
AND THE FLAMES BLOCK THE WAY TO THE STAIRS!
SPLENDID! THE CHEF HAS STARTED MAKING THE MEAL.
FIRE!
THE KING IS IN THE TOWER!
WE'LL BURN INTO BACON!
DID SOMEONE MENTION BACON?

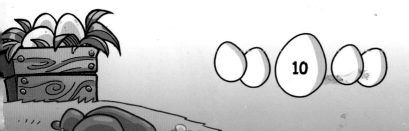

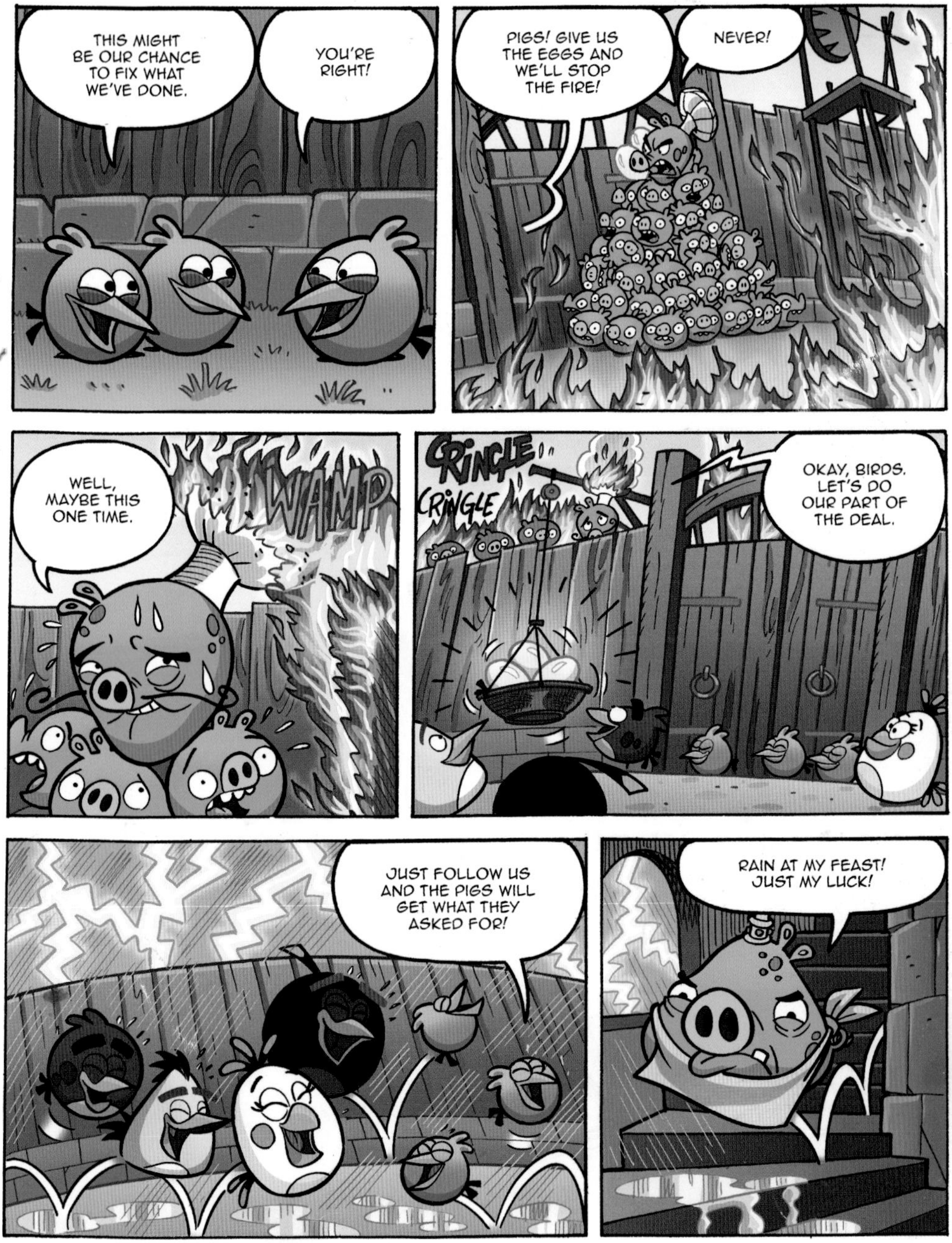
THIS MIGHT BE OUR CHANCE TO FIX WHAT WE'VE DONE.
YOU'RE RIGHT!
PIGS! GIVE US THE EGGS AND WE'LL STOP THE FIRE!
NEVER!
WELL, MAYBE THIS ONE TIME.
WAMP
CRINGLE
CRINGLE
OKAY, BIRDS. LET'S DO OUR PART OF THE DEAL.
JUST FOLLOW US AND THE PIGS WILL GET WHAT THEY ASKED FOR!
RAIN AT MY FEAST! JUST MY LUCK!

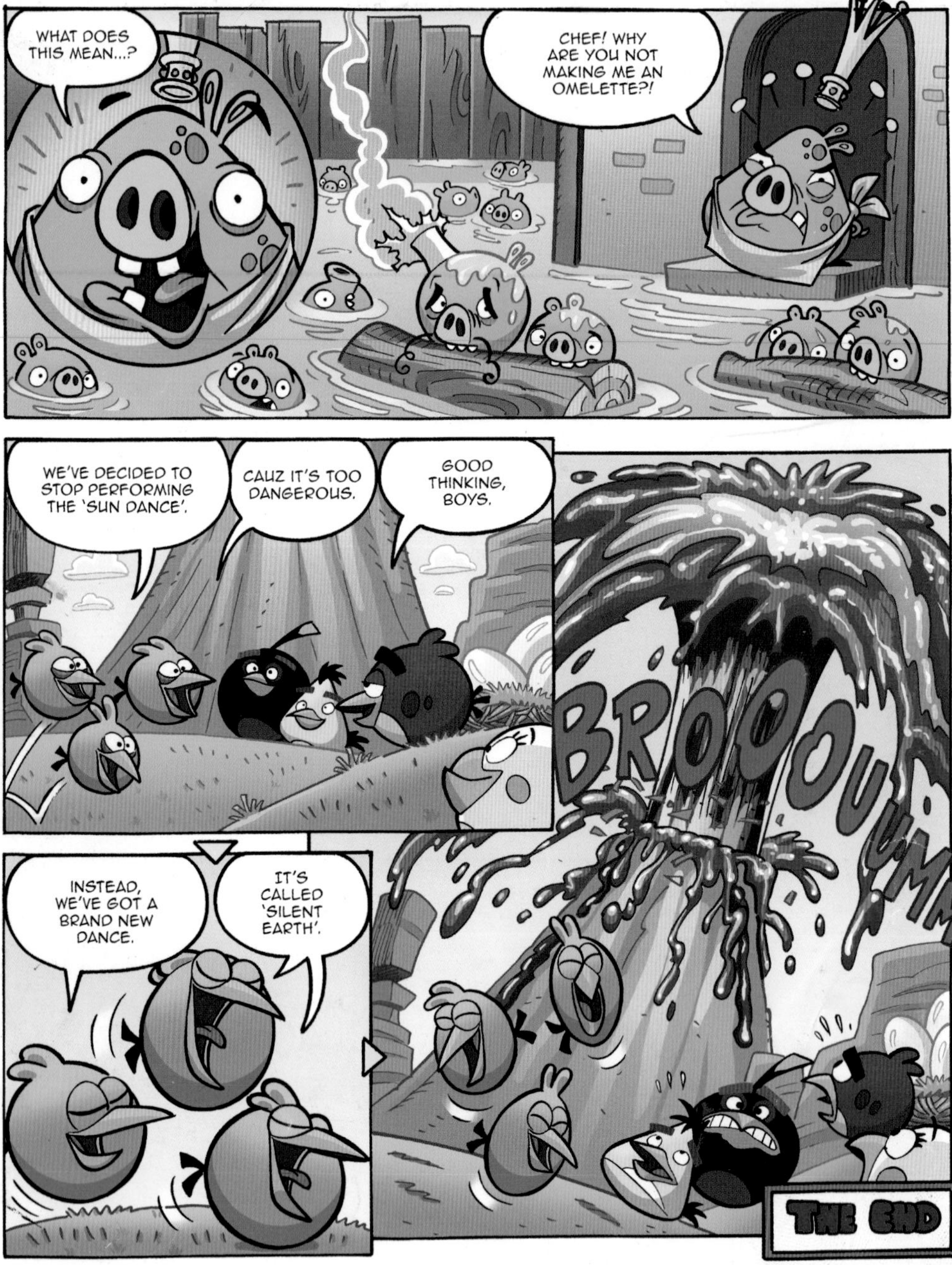
WHAT DOES THIS MEAN...?
CHEF! WHY ARE YOU NOT MAKING ME AN OMELETTE?!
WE'VE DECIDED TO STOP PERFORMING THE 'SUN DANCE'.
CAUZ IT'S TOO DANGEROUS.
GOOD THINKING, BOYS.
INSTEAD, WE'VE GOT A BRAND NEW DANCE.
IT'S CALLED 'SILENT EARTH'.
BROOOOUUMM
THE END

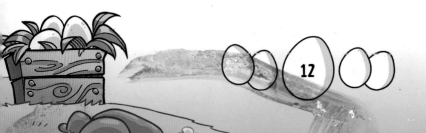

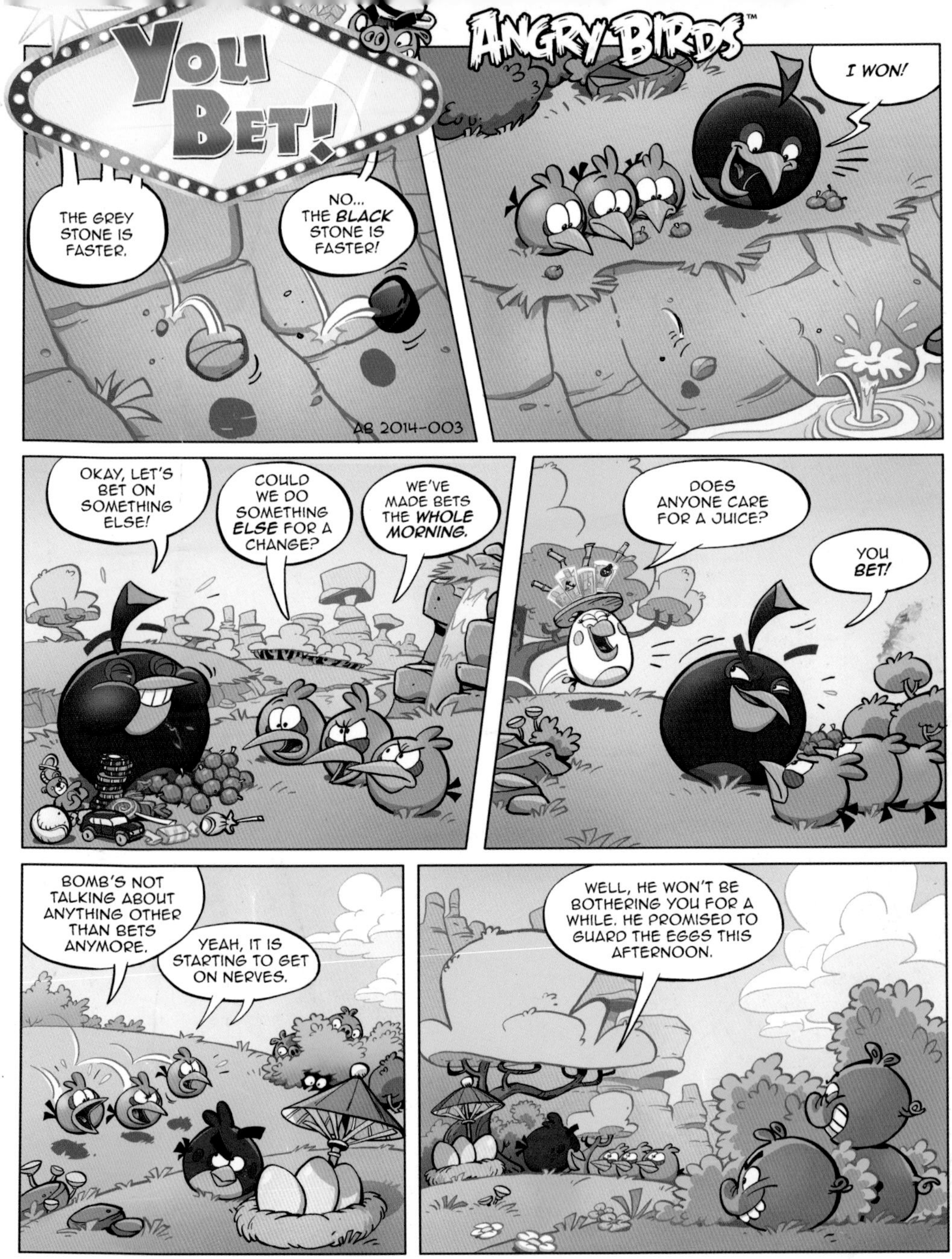
ANGRY BIRDS™
YOU BET!
THE GREY STONE IS FASTER.
NO... THE BLACK STONE IS FASTER!
AB 2014-003
I WON!
OKAY, LET'S BET ON SOMETHING ELSE!
COULD WE DO SOMETHING ELSE FOR A CHANGE?
WE'VE MADE BETS THE WHOLE MORNING.
DOES ANYONE CARE FOR A JUICE?
YOU BET!
BOMB'S NOT TALKING ABOUT ANYTHING OTHER THAN BETS ANYMORE.
YEAH, IT IS STARTING TO GET ON NERVES.
WELL, HE WON'T BE BOTHERING YOU FOR A WHILE. HE PROMISED TO GUARD THE EGGS THIS AFTERNOON.

WRITTEN BY: JANNE TORISEVA • ART BY: THOMAS CABELLIC • COLORS BY: DIGIKORE • LETTERS BY: PISARA OY

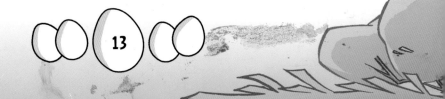

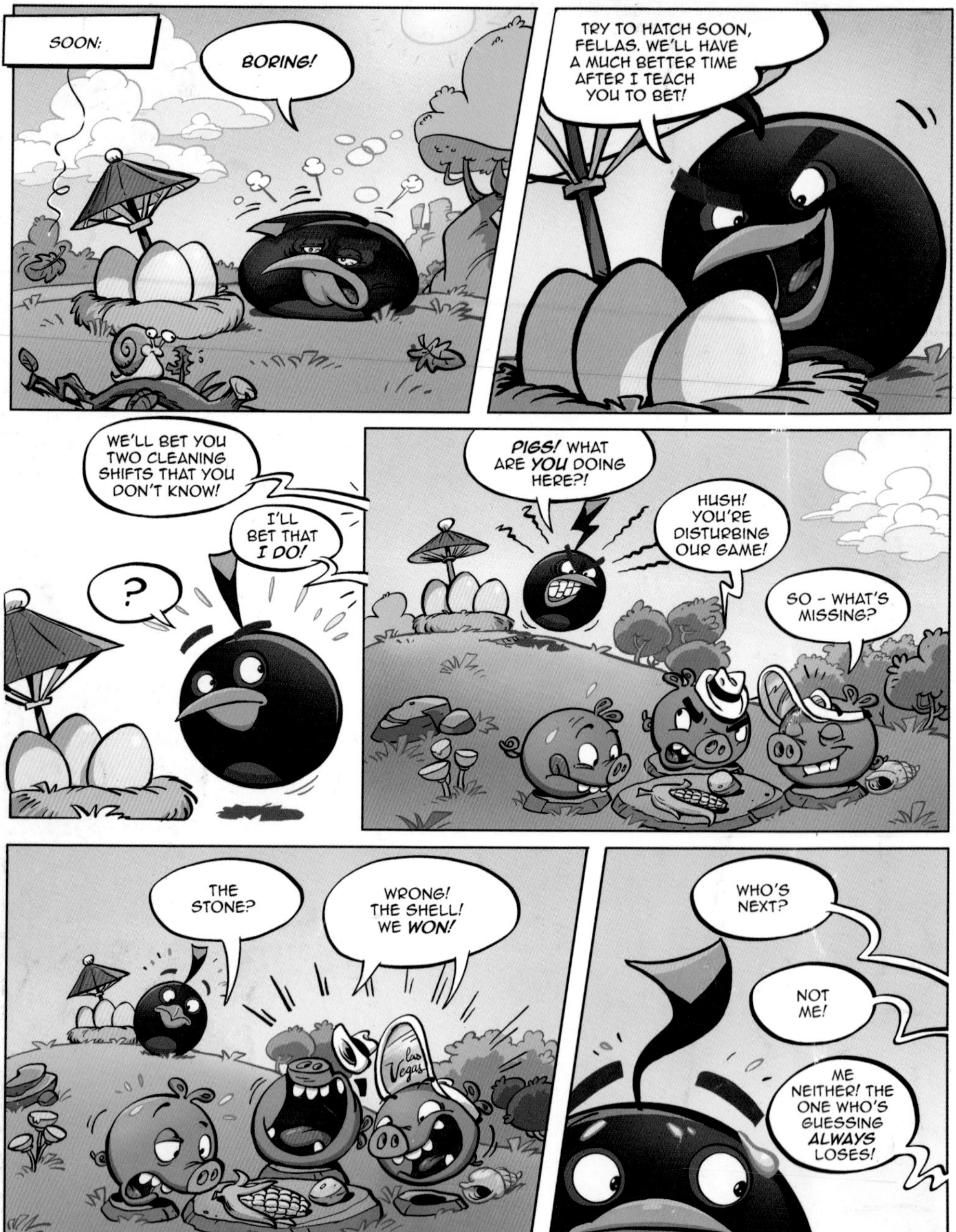
SOON:
BORING!
TRY TO HATCH SOON, FELLAS. WE'LL HAVE A MUCH BETTER TIME AFTER I TEACH YOU TO BET!
WE'LL BET YOU TWO CLEANING SHIFTS THAT YOU DON'T KNOW!
?
I'LL BET THAT I DO!
PIGS! WHAT ARE YOU DOING HERE?!
HUSH! YOU'RE DISTURBING OUR GAME!
SO - WHAT'S MISSING?
THE STONE?
WRONG! THE SHELL! WE WON!
Las Vegas
WHO'S NEXT?
NOT ME!
ME NEITHER! THE ONE WHO'S GUESSING ALWAYS LOSES!

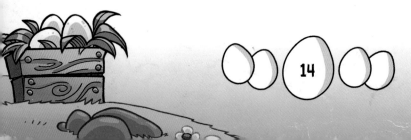

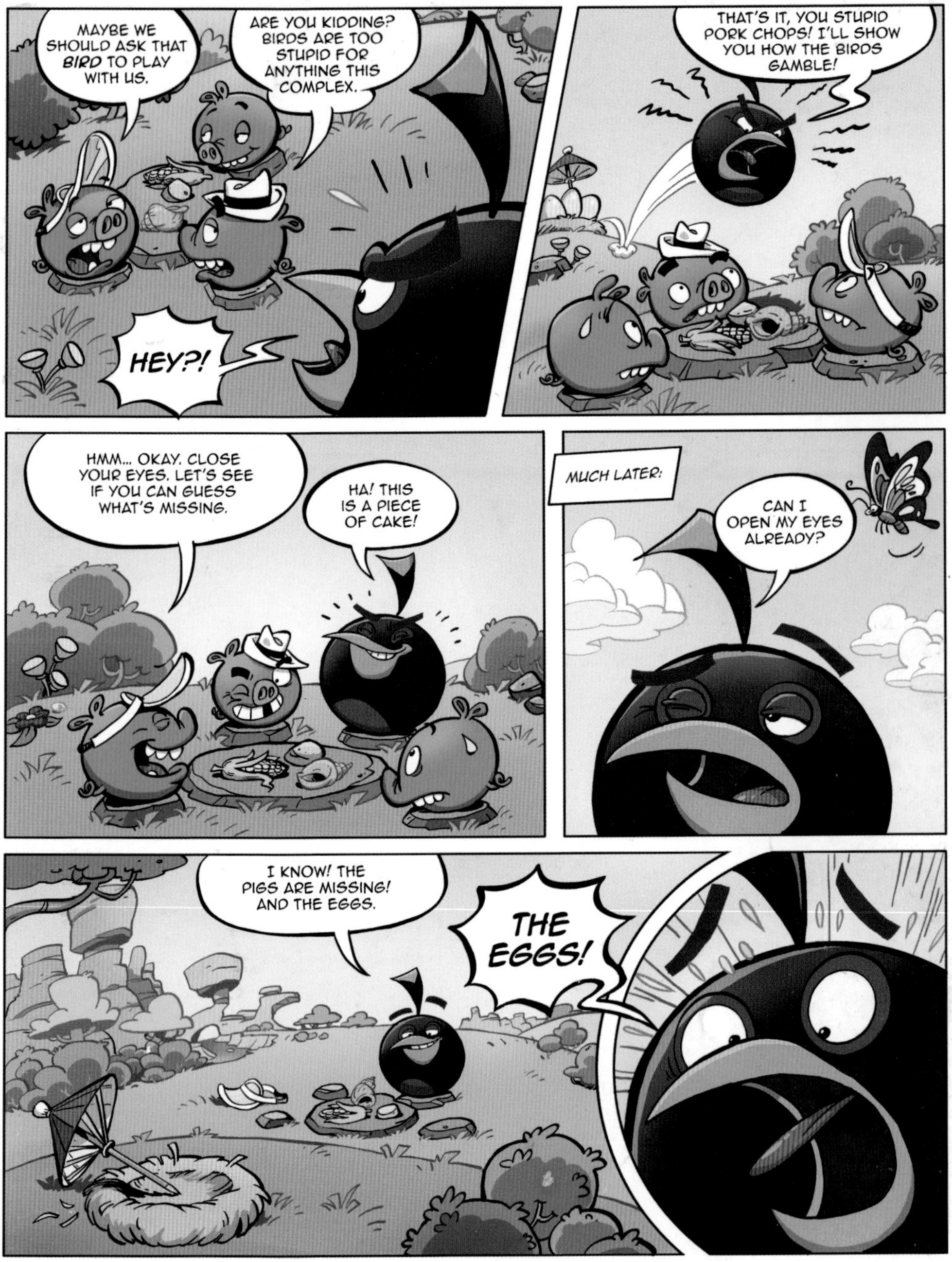

MAYBE WE SHOULD ASK THAT BIRD TO PLAY WITH US.
ARE YOU KIDDING? BIRDS ARE TOO STUPID FOR ANYTHING THIS COMPLEX.
HEY?!
THAT'S IT, YOU STUPID PORK CHOPS! I'LL SHOW YOU HOW THE BIRDS GAMBLE!
HMM... OKAY. CLOSE YOUR EYES. LET'S SEE IF YOU CAN GUESS WHAT'S MISSING.
HA! THIS IS A PIECE OF CAKE!
MUCH LATER:
CAN I OPEN MY EYES ALREADY?
I KNOW! THE PIGS ARE MISSING! AND THE EGGS.
THE EGGS!

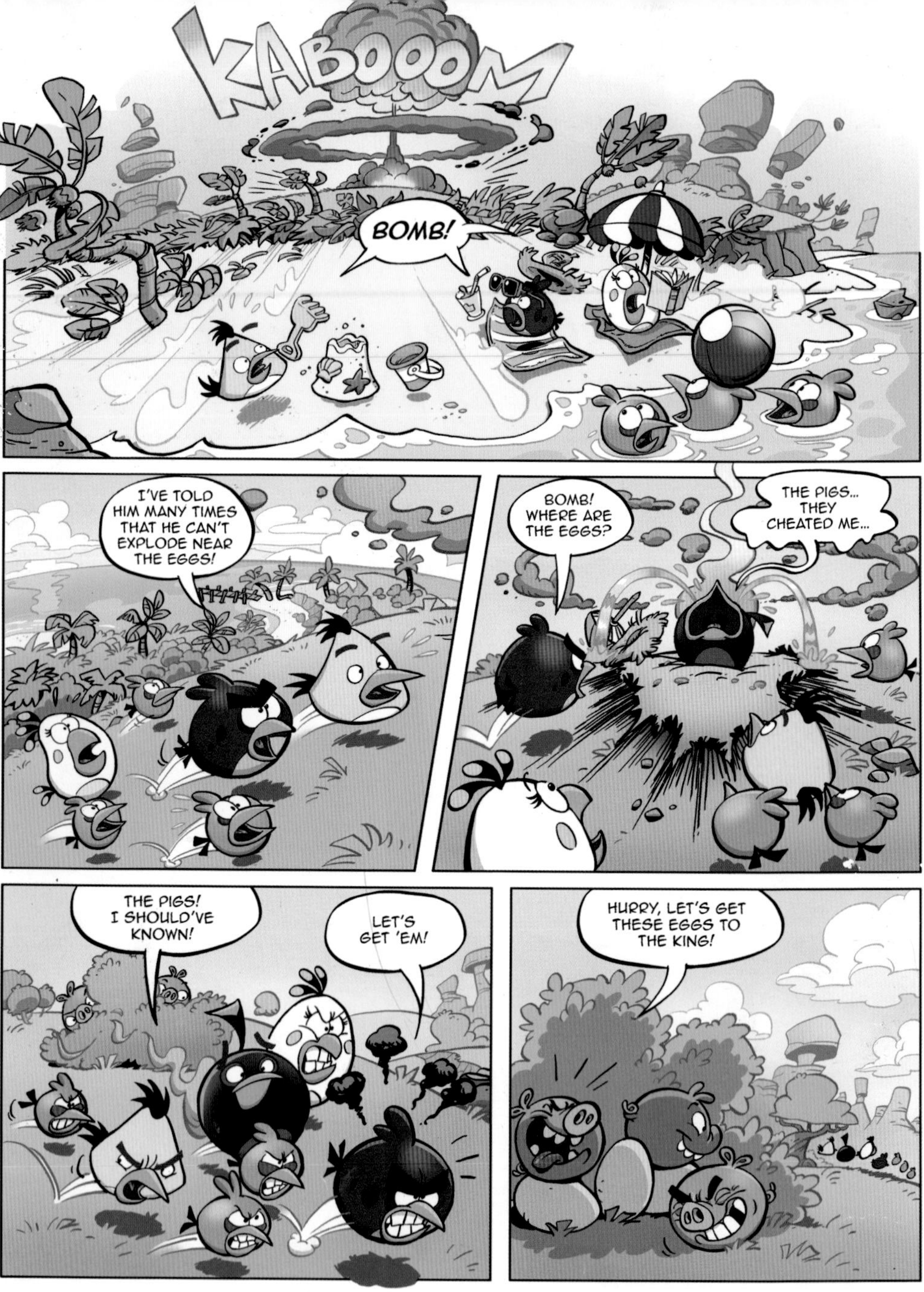
KABOOOM
BOMB!
I'VE TOLD HIM MANY TIMES THAT HE CAN'T EXPLODE NEAR THE EGGS!
BOMB! WHERE ARE THE EGGS?
THE PIGS... THEY CHEATED ME...
THE PIGS! I SHOULD'VE KNOWN!
LET'S GET 'EM!
HURRY, LET'S GET THESE EGGS TO THE KING!

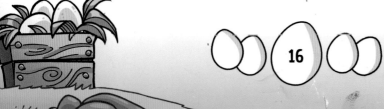

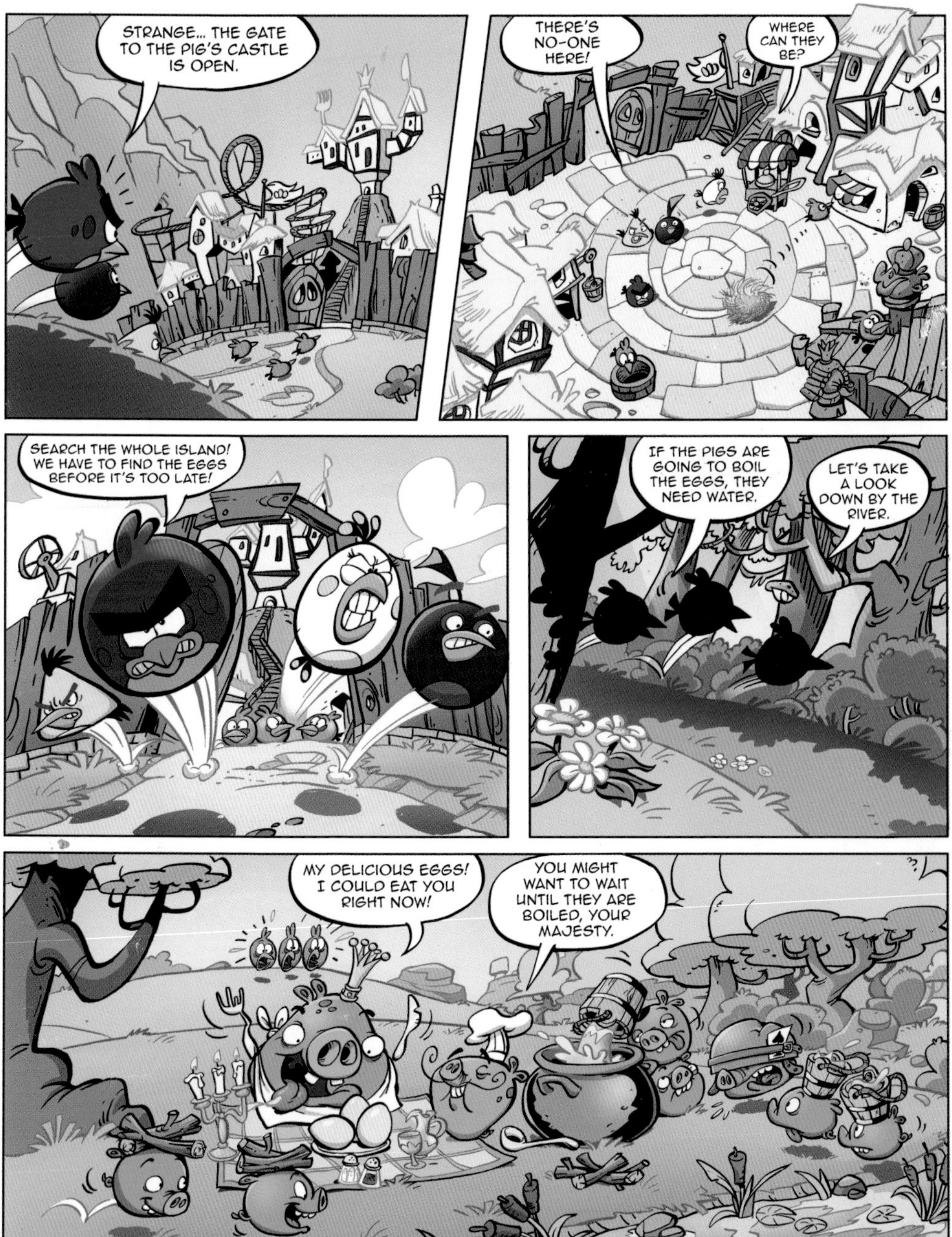

STRANGE... THE GATE TO THE PIG'S CASTLE IS OPEN.
THERE'S NO-ONE HERE!
WHERE CAN THEY BE?
SEARCH THE WHOLE ISLAND! WE HAVE TO FIND THE EGGS BEFORE IT'S TOO LATE!
IF THE PIGS ARE GOING TO BOIL THE EGGS, THEY NEED WATER.
LET'S TAKE A LOOK DOWN BY THE RIVER.
MY DELICIOUS EGGS! I COULD EAT YOU RIGHT NOW!
YOU MIGHT WANT TO WAIT UNTIL THEY ARE BOILED, YOUR MAJESTY.

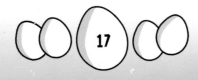

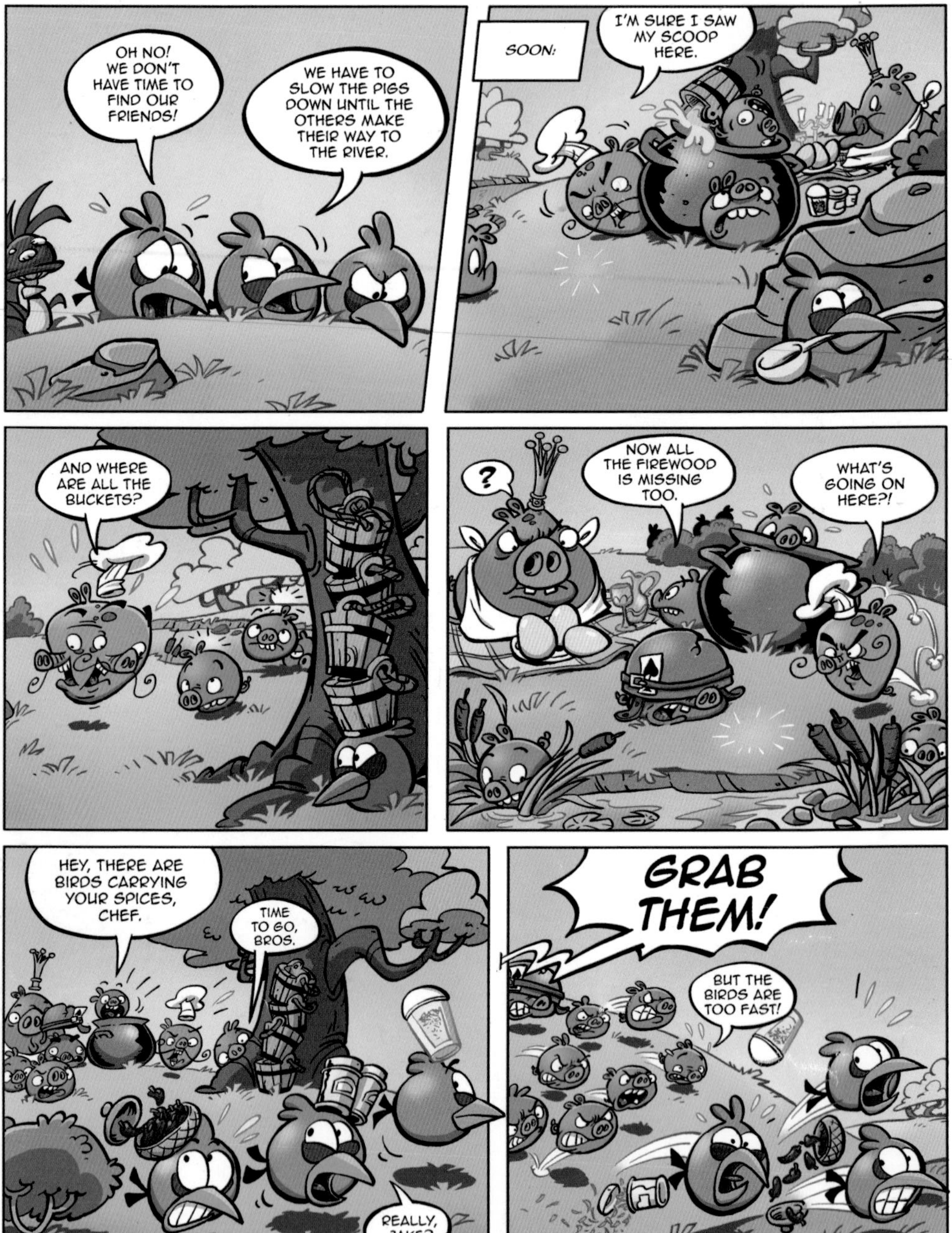
OH NO! WE DON'T HAVE TIME TO FIND OUR FRIENDS!
WE HAVE TO SLOW THE PIGS DOWN UNTIL THE OTHERS MAKE THEIR WAY TO THE RIVER.
SOON:
I'M SURE I SAW MY SCOOP HERE.
AND WHERE ARE ALL THE BUCKETS?
?
NOW ALL THE FIREWOOD IS MISSING TOO.
WHAT'S GOING ON HERE?!
HEY, THERE ARE BIRDS CARRYING YOUR SPICES, CHEF.
TIME TO GO, BROS.
REALLY, JAKE?
GRAB THEM!
BUT THE BIRDS ARE TOO FAST!

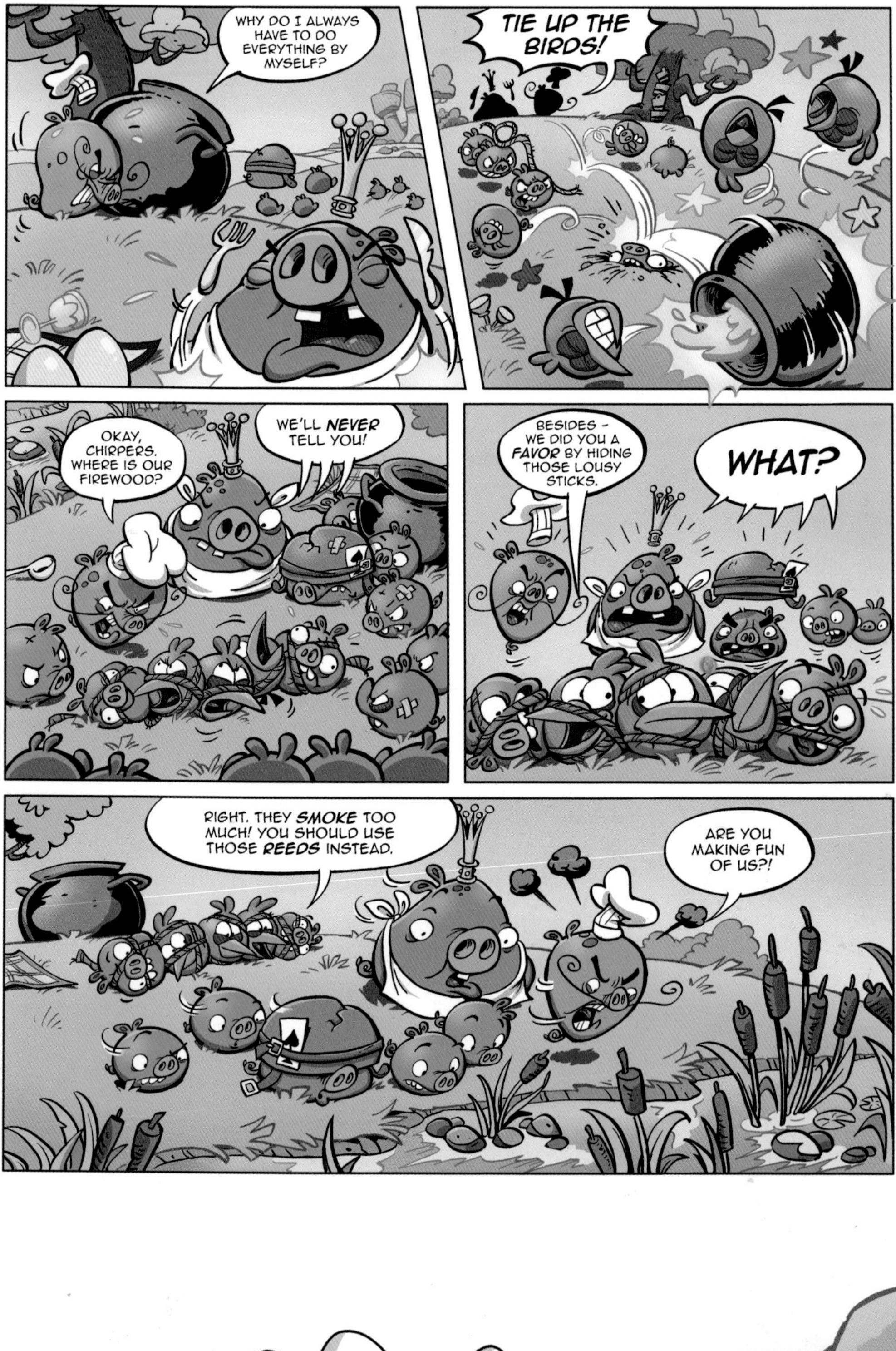
WHY DO I ALWAYS HAVE TO DO EVERYTHING BY MYSELF?
TIE UP THE BIRDS!
OKAY, CHIRPERS. WHERE IS OUR FIREWOOD?
WE'LL NEVER TELL YOU!
BESIDES - WE DID YOU A FAVOR BY HIDING THOSE LOUSY STICKS.
WHAT?
RIGHT. THEY SMOKE TOO MUCH! YOU SHOULD USE THOSE REEDS INSTEAD.
ARE YOU MAKING FUN OF US?!

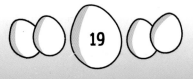

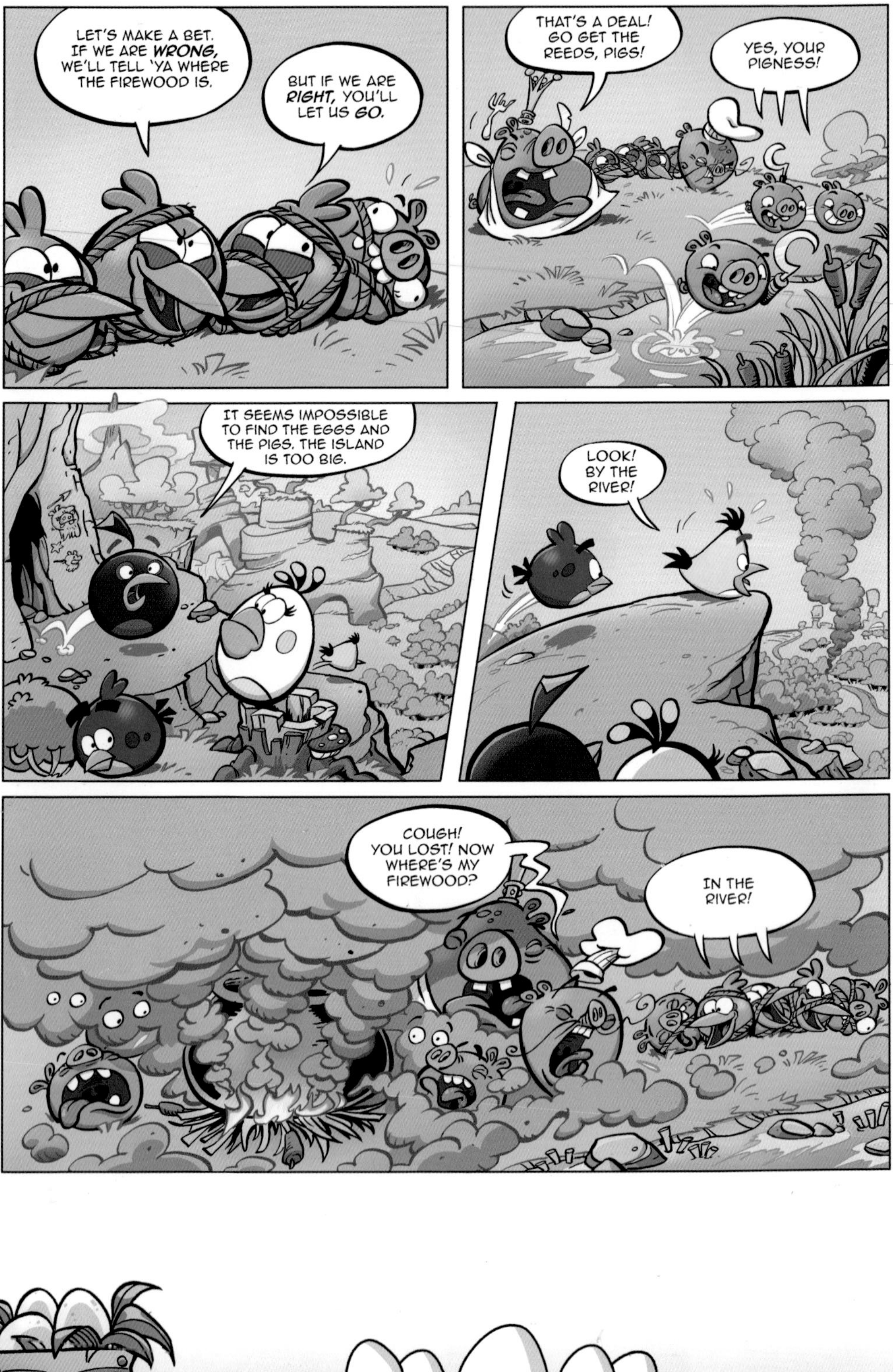
LET'S MAKE A BET. IF WE ARE **WRONG,** WE'LL TELL 'YA WHERE THE FIREWOOD IS.
BUT IF WE ARE **RIGHT,** YOU'LL LET US **GO.**
THAT'S A DEAL! GO GET THE REEDS, PIGS!
YES, YOUR PIGNESS!
IT SEEMS IMPOSSIBLE TO FIND THE EGGS AND THE PIGS. THE ISLAND IS TOO BIG.
LOOK! BY THE RIVER!
COUGH! YOU LOST! NOW WHERE'S MY FIREWOOD?
IN THE RIVER!

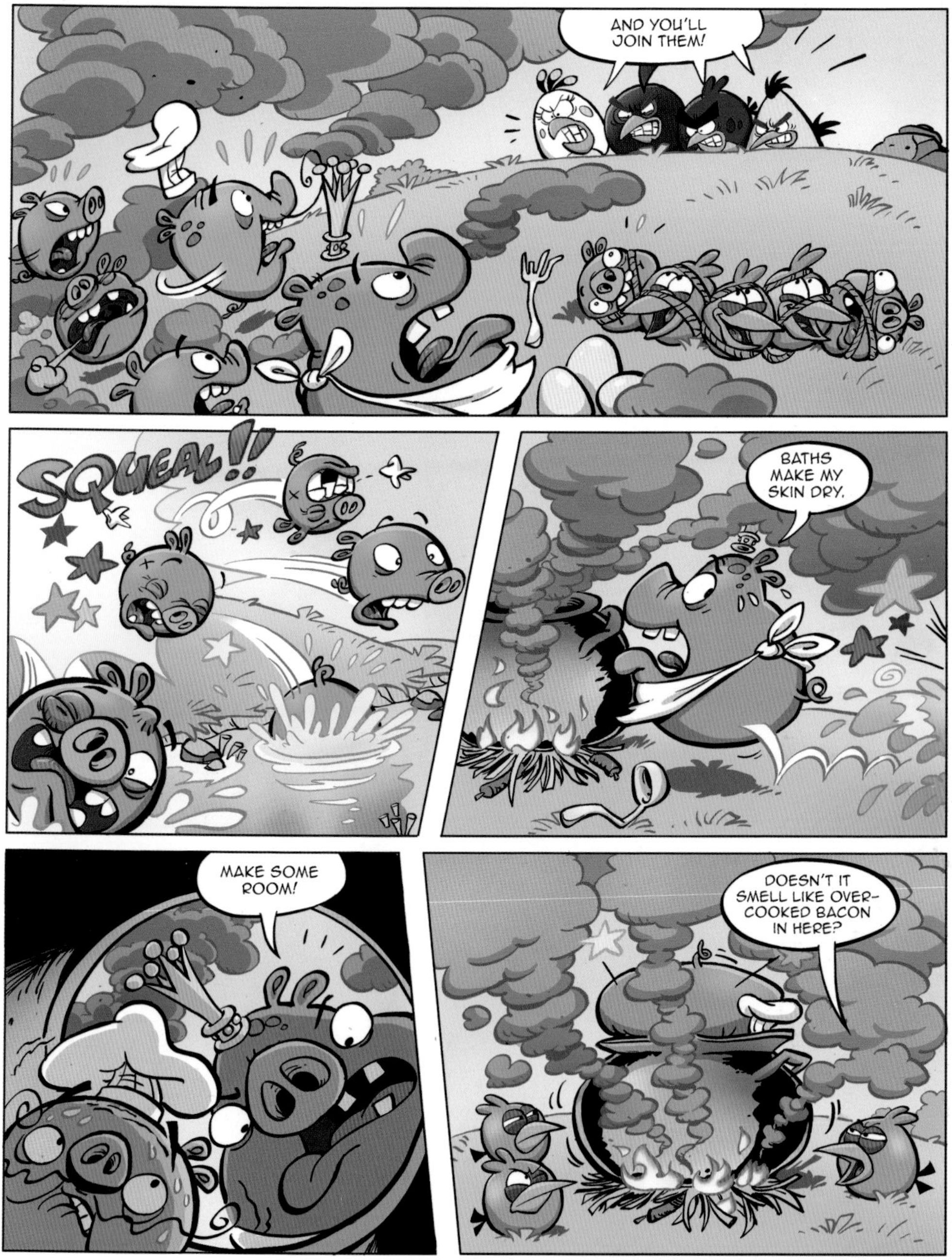
AND YOU'LL JOIN THEM!
SQUEAL!!
BATHS MAKE MY SKIN DRY.
MAKE SOME ROOM!
DOESN'T IT SMELL LIKE OVER-COOKED BACON IN HERE?

I THINK THIS ROAST IS *DONE!*
BLUB! HELP! I CAN'T SWIM!
ME NEITHER!
BE QUIET! THE WATER DOESN'T EVEN REACH YOUR SNOUT!
GOOD JOB, BOYS!
AND NO MORE GAMBLING, BOMB.
ALL RIGHT.
MAYBE THE PIGS WILL FORGET THE EGGS NOW FOR A WHILE.
FORGET THE EGGS? I DOUBT IT!
YEAH! I'LL *BET* THAT THEY ARE MAKING NEW PLANS FOR THE EGGS ALREADY!
THE END

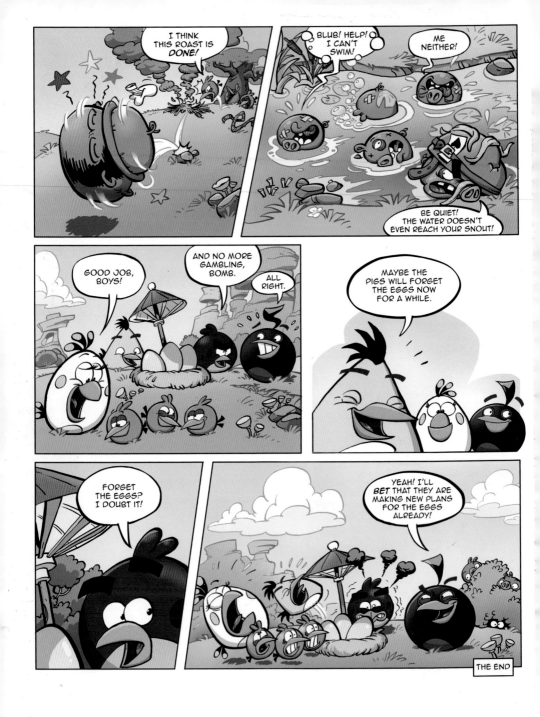

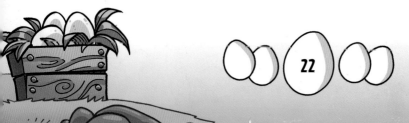

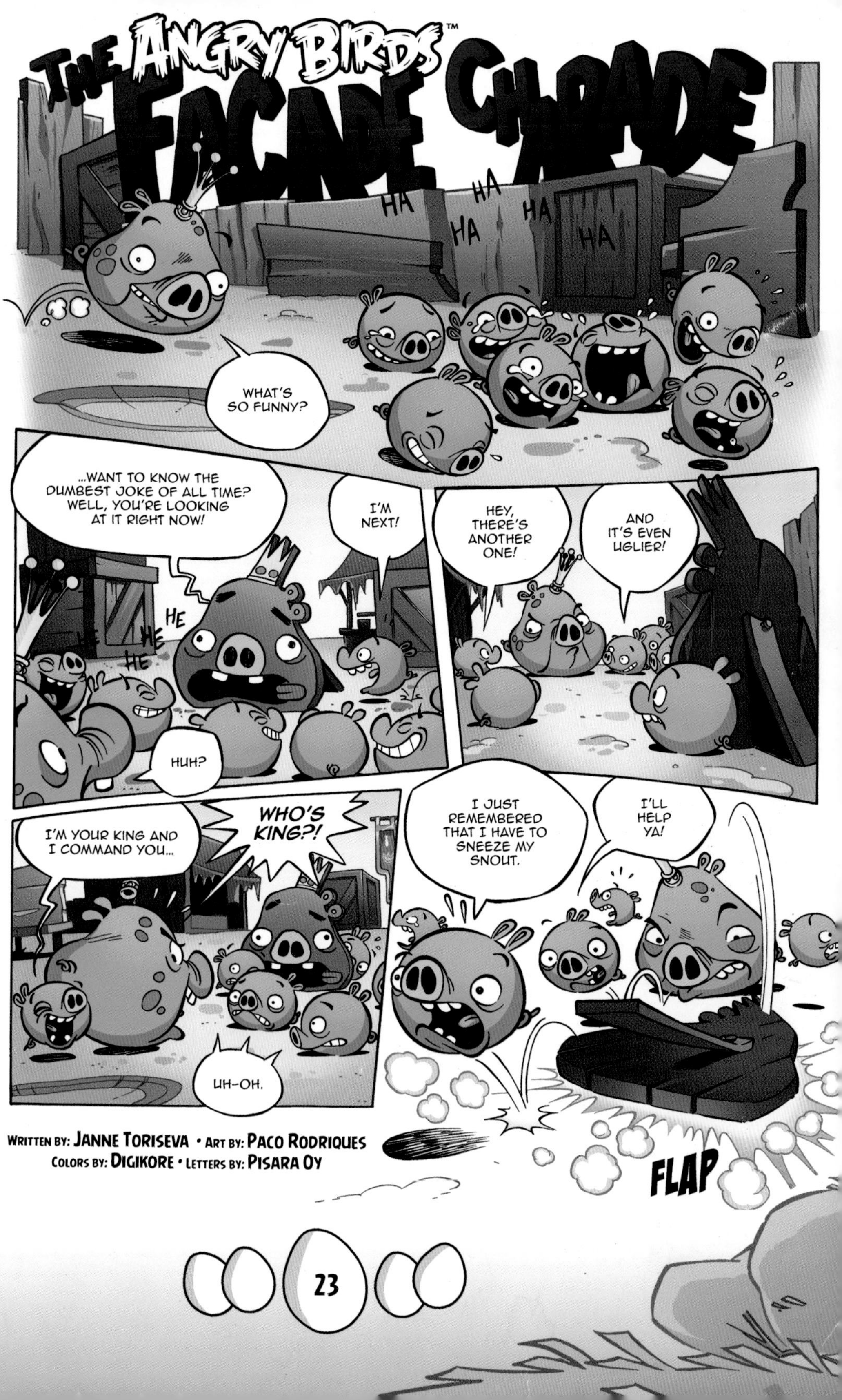
THE ANGRY BIRDS FACADE CHARADE
HA HA HA HA HA
WHAT'S SO FUNNY?
...WANT TO KNOW THE DUMBEST JOKE OF ALL TIME? WELL, YOU'RE LOOKING AT IT RIGHT NOW!
I'M NEXT!
HE HE HE HE
HUH?
HEY, THERE'S ANOTHER ONE!
AND IT'S EVEN UGLIER!
I'M YOUR KING AND I COMMAND YOU...
WHO'S KING?!
UH-OH.
I JUST REMEMBERED THAT I HAVE TO SNEEZE MY SNOUT.
I'LL HELP YA!
FLAP

WRITTEN BY: JANNE TORISEVA • ART BY: PACO RODRIQUES
COLORS BY: DIGIKORE • LETTERS BY: PISARA OY

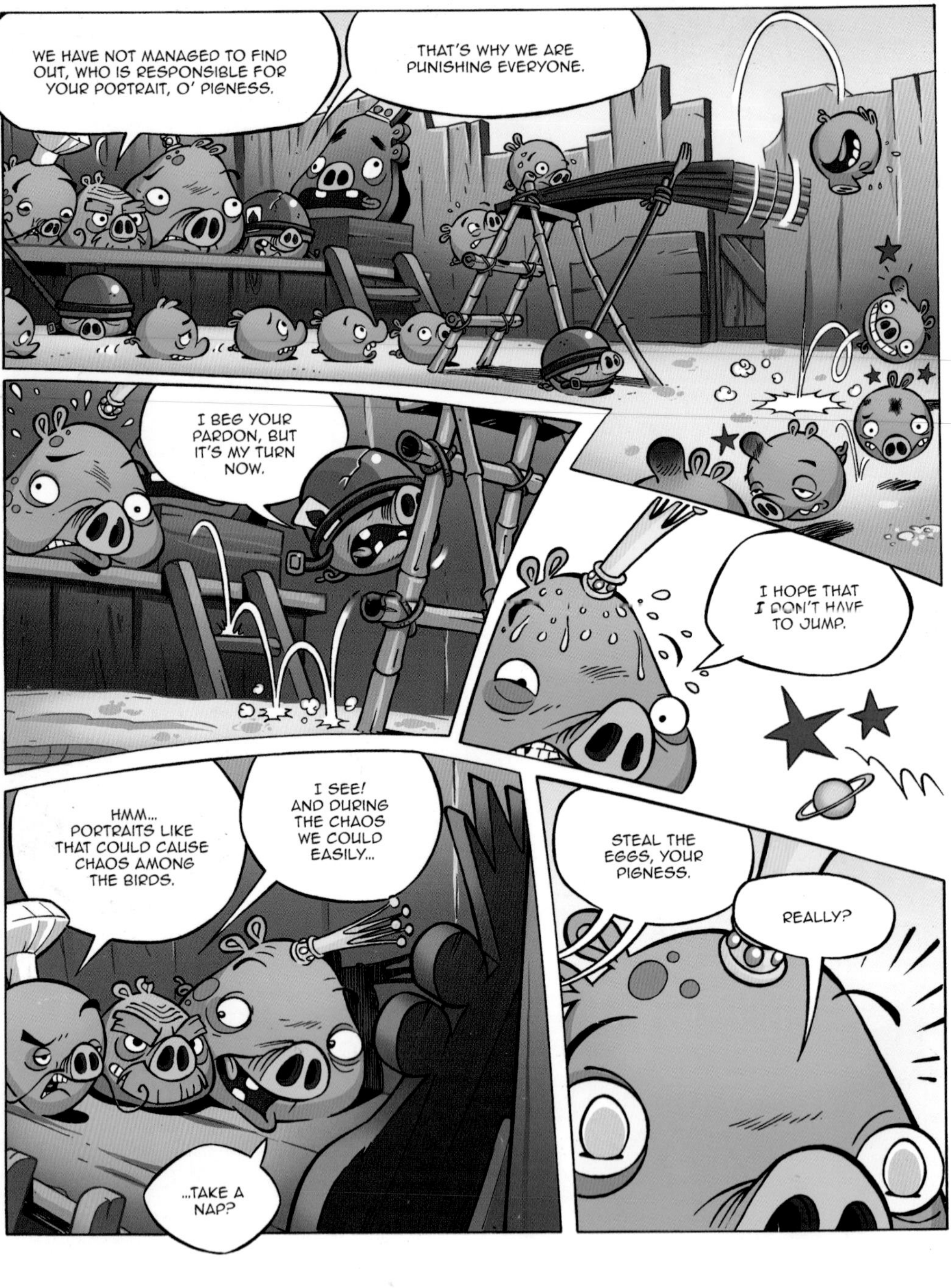
WE HAVE NOT MANAGED TO FIND OUT, WHO IS RESPONSIBLE FOR YOUR PORTRAIT, O' PIGNESS.
THAT'S WHY WE ARE PUNISHING EVERYONE.
I BEG YOUR PARDON, BUT IT'S MY TURN NOW.
I HOPE THAT I DON'T HAVE TO JUMP.
HMM... PORTRAITS LIKE THAT COULD CAUSE CHAOS AMONG THE BIRDS.
I SEE! AND DURING THE CHAOS WE COULD EASILY...
...TAKE A NAP?
STEAL THE EGGS, YOUR PIGNESS.
REALLY?

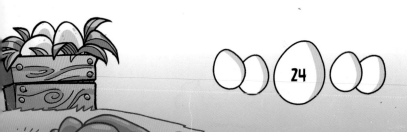

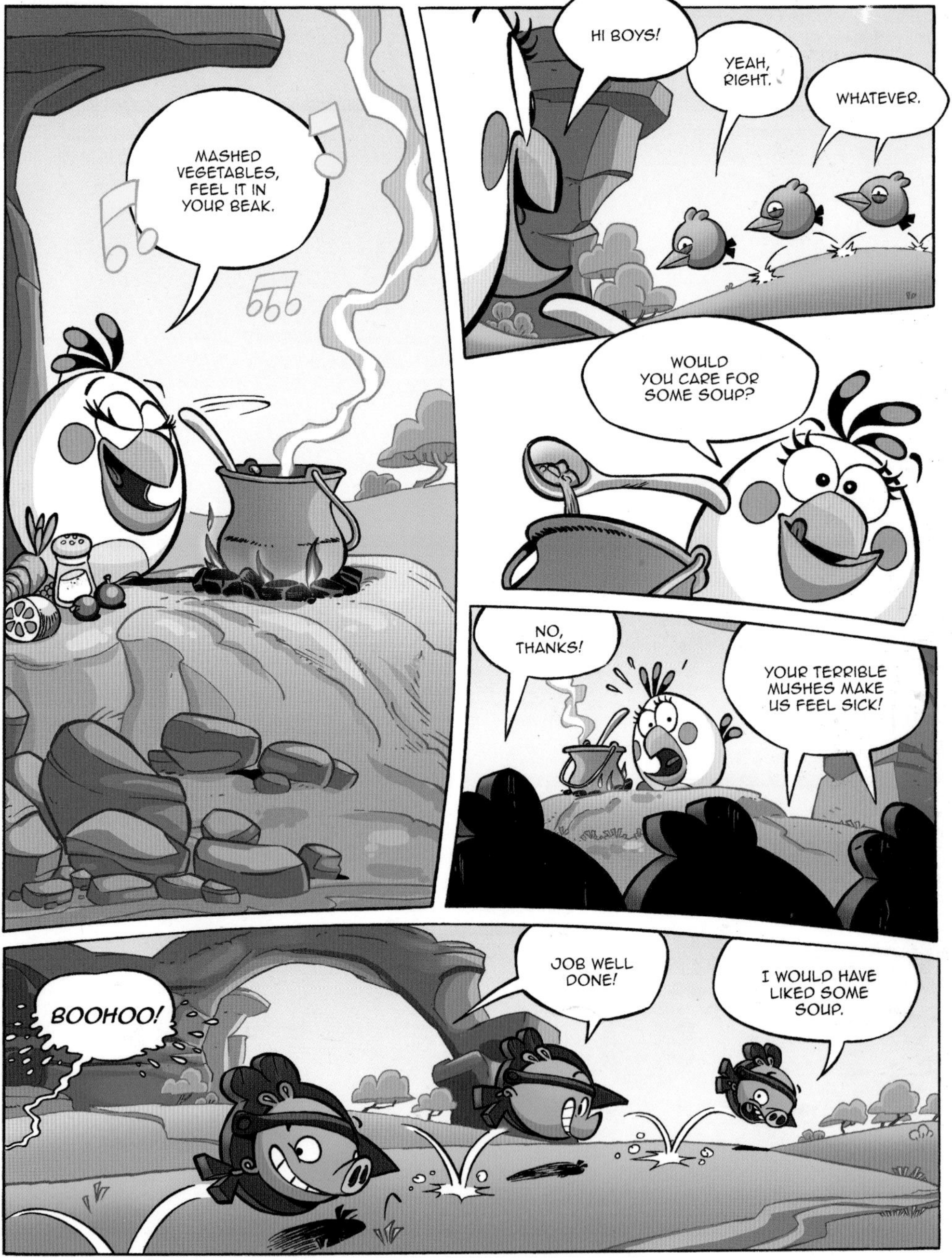
MASHED VEGETABLES, FEEL IT IN YOUR BEAK.
HI BOYS!
YEAH, RIGHT.
WHATEVER.
WOULD YOU CARE FOR SOME SOUP?
NO, THANKS!
YOUR TERRIBLE MUSHES MAKE US FEEL SICK!
BOOHOO!
JOB WELL DONE!
I WOULD HAVE LIKED SOME SOUP.

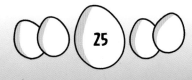

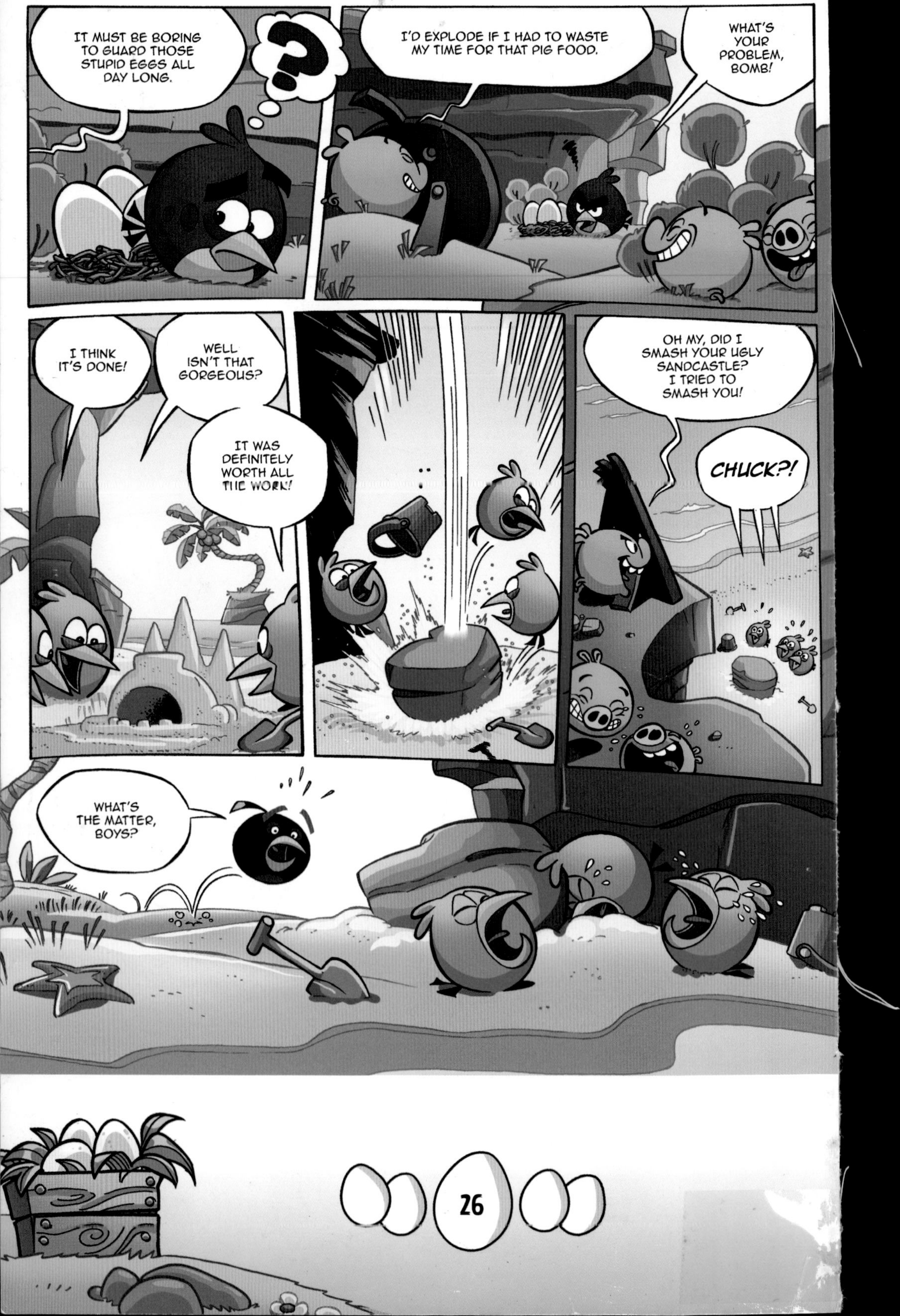
IT MUST BE BORING TO GUARD THOSE STUPID EGGS ALL DAY LONG.
?
I'D EXPLODE IF I HAD TO WASTE MY TIME FOR THAT PIG FOOD.
WHAT'S YOUR PROBLEM, BOMB!
I THINK IT'S DONE!
WELL ISN'T THAT GORGEOUS?
IT WAS DEFINITELY WORTH ALL THE WORK!
OH MY, DID I SMASH YOUR UGLY SANDCASTLE? I TRIED TO SMASH YOU!
CHUCK?!
WHAT'S THE MATTER, BOYS?

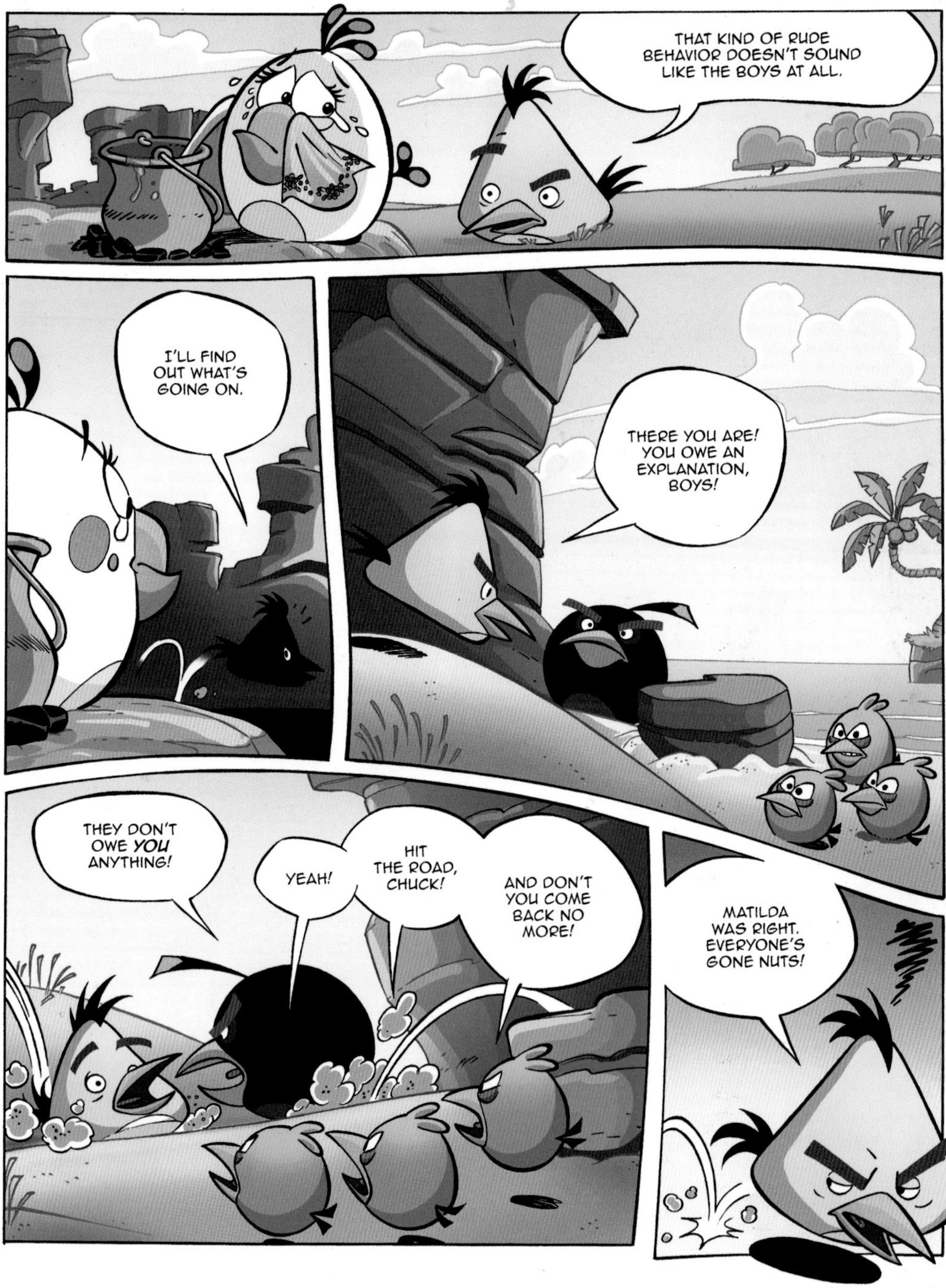
THAT KIND OF RUDE BEHAVIOR DOESN'T SOUND LIKE THE BOYS AT ALL.
I'LL FIND OUT WHAT'S GOING ON.
THERE YOU ARE! YOU OWE AN EXPLANATION, BOYS!
THEY DON'T OWE *YOU* ANYTHING!
YEAH!
HIT THE ROAD, CHUCK!
AND DON'T YOU COME BACK NO MORE!
MATILDA WAS RIGHT. EVERYONE'S GONE NUTS!

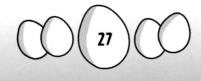

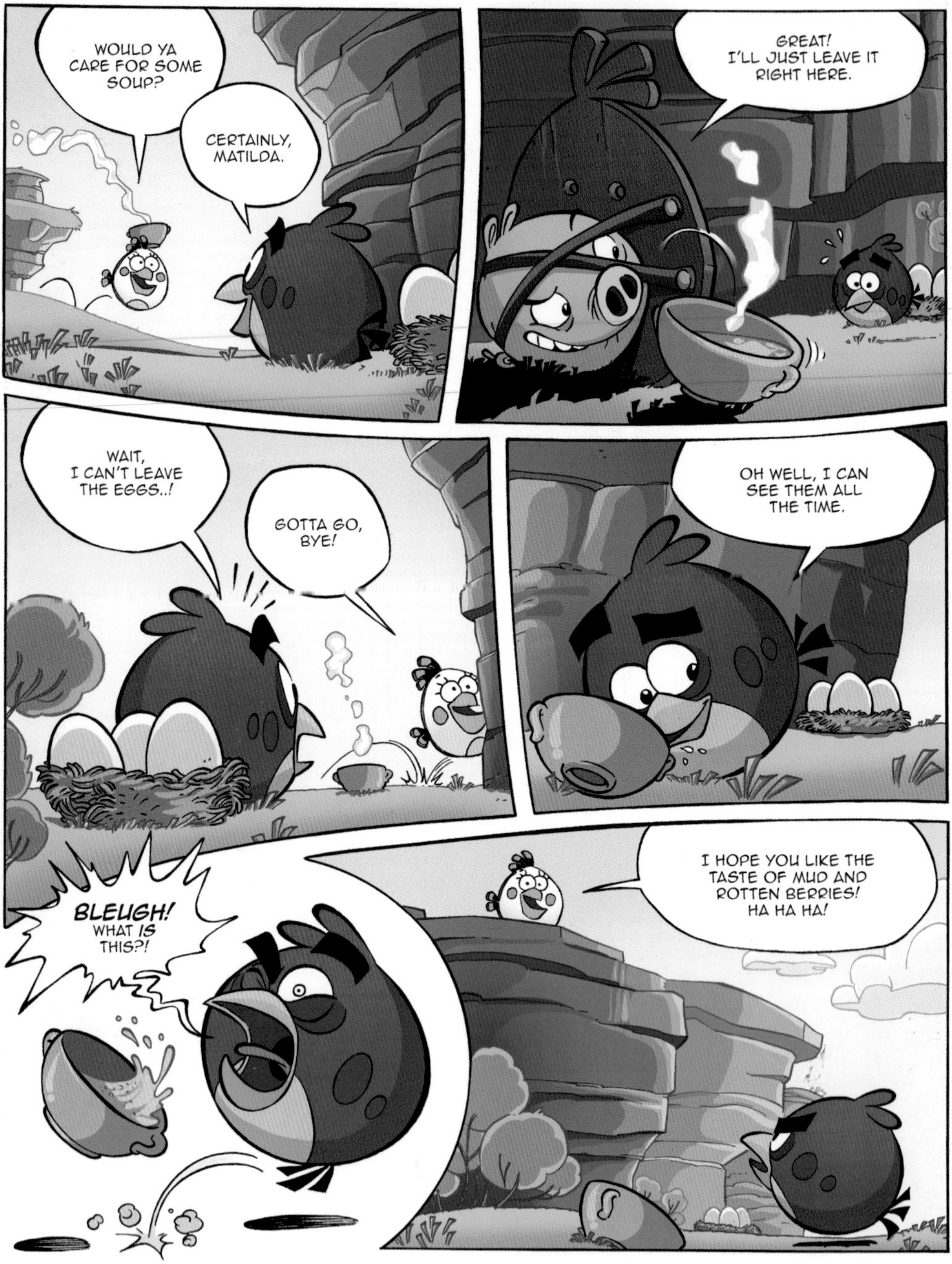
WOULD YA CARE FOR SOME SOUP?
CERTAINLY, MATILDA.
GREAT! I'LL JUST LEAVE IT RIGHT HERE.
WAIT, I CAN'T LEAVE THE EGGS..!
GOTTA GO, BYE!
OH WELL, I CAN SEE THEM ALL THE TIME.
BLEUGH! WHAT IS THIS?!
I HOPE YOU LIKE THE TASTE OF MUD AND ROTTEN BERRIES! HA HA HA!

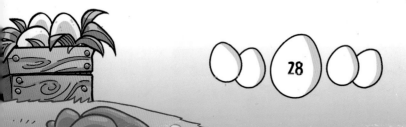

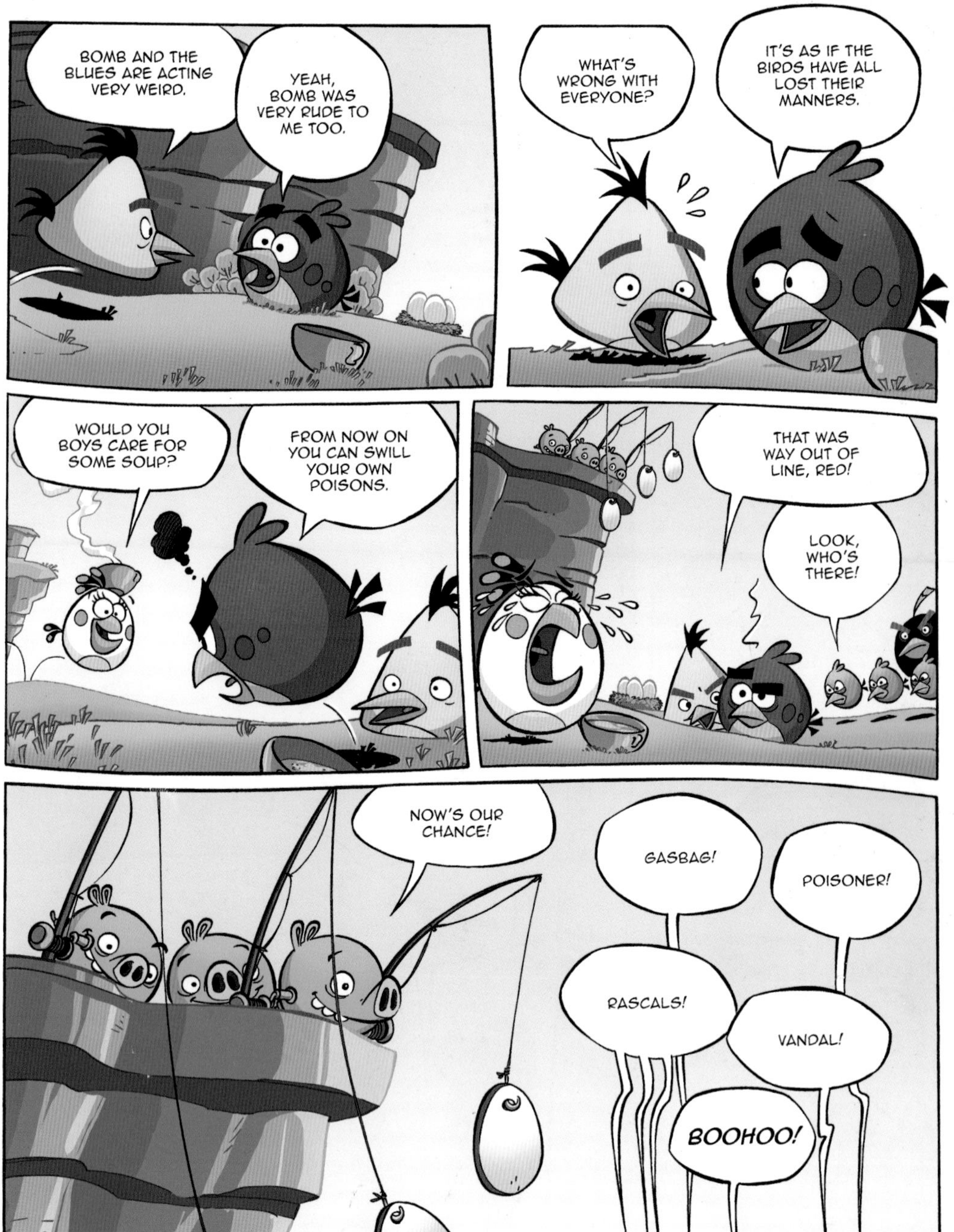
BOMB AND THE BLUES ARE ACTING VERY WEIRD.
YEAH, BOMB WAS VERY RUDE TO ME TOO.
WHAT'S WRONG WITH EVERYONE?
IT'S AS IF THE BIRDS HAVE ALL LOST THEIR MANNERS.
WOULD YOU BOYS CARE FOR SOME SOUP?
FROM NOW ON YOU CAN SWILL YOUR OWN POISONS.
THAT WAS WAY OUT OF LINE, RED!
LOOK, WHO'S THERE!
NOW'S OUR CHANCE!
GASBAG!
POISONER!
RASCALS!
VANDAL!
BOOHOO!

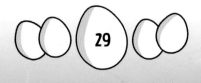

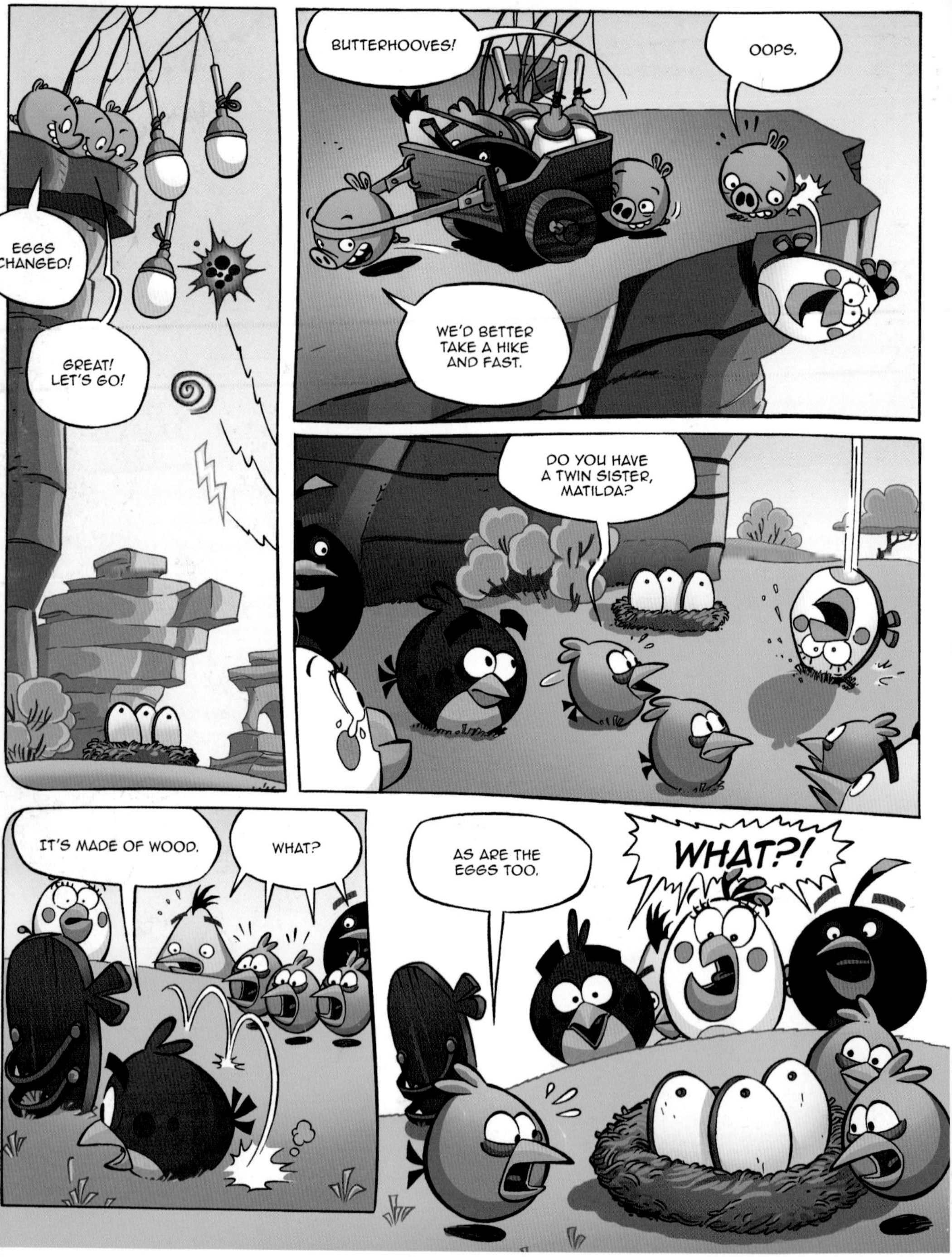
EGGS CHANGED!
GREAT! LET'S GO!
BUTTERHOOVES!
OOPS.
WE'D BETTER TAKE A HIKE AND FAST.
DO YOU HAVE A TWIN SISTER, MATILDA?
IT'S MADE OF WOOD.
WHAT?
AS ARE THE EGGS TOO.
WHAT?!

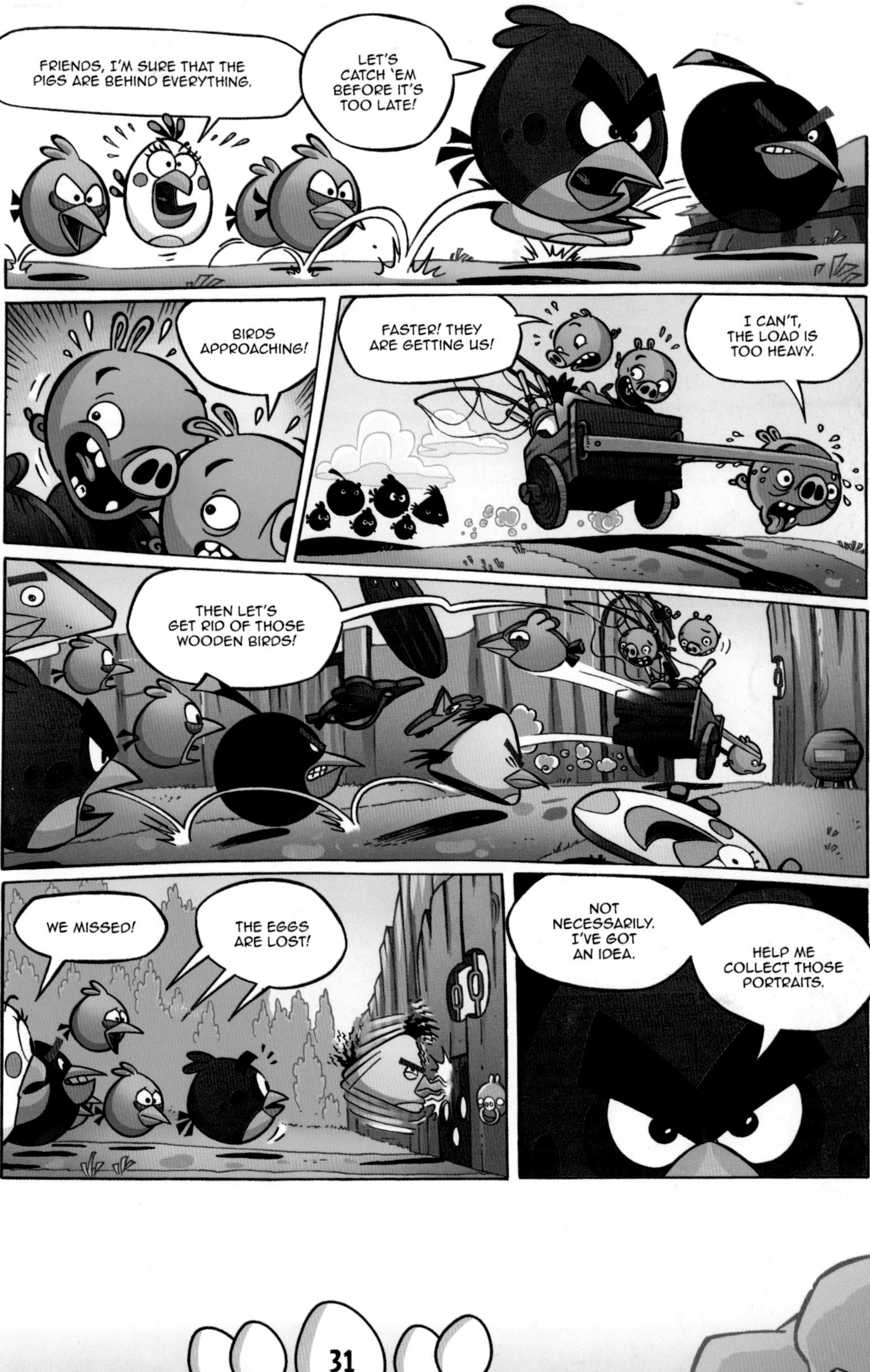
FRIENDS, I'M SURE THAT THE PIGS ARE BEHIND EVERYTHING.
LET'S CATCH 'EM BEFORE IT'S TOO LATE!
BIRDS APPROACHING!
FASTER! THEY ARE GETTING US!
I CAN'T, THE LOAD IS TOO HEAVY.
THEN LET'S GET RID OF THOSE WOODEN BIRDS!
WE MISSED!
THE EGGS ARE LOST!
NOT NECESSARILY. I'VE GOT AN IDEA.
HELP ME COLLECT THOSE PORTRAITS.

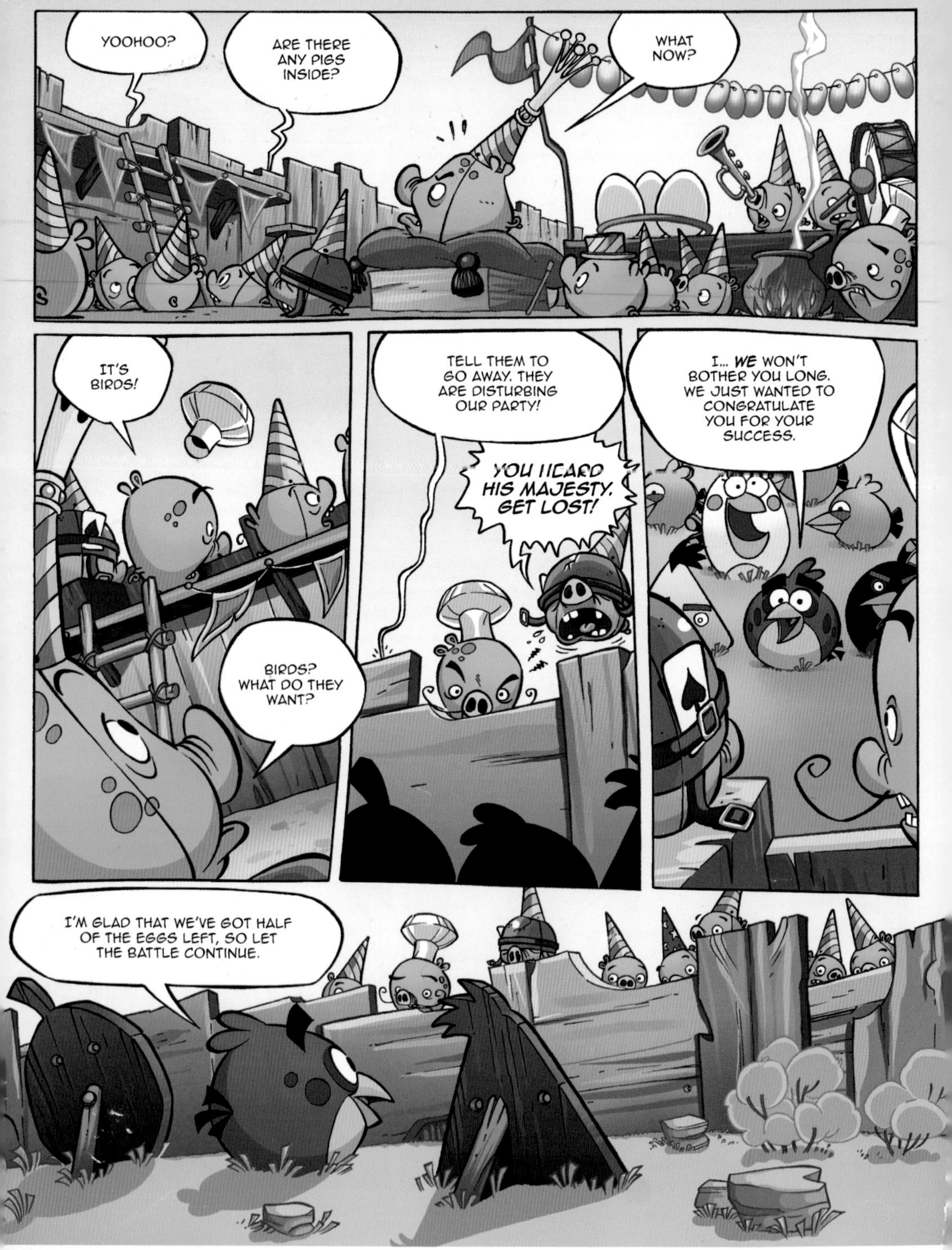
YOOHOO?
ARE THERE ANY PIGS INSIDE?
WHAT NOW?
IT'S BIRDS!
BIRDS? WHAT DO THEY WANT?
TELL THEM TO GO AWAY. THEY ARE DISTURBING OUR PARTY!
YOU HEARD HIS MAJESTY. GET LOST!
I... *WE* WON'T BOTHER YOU LONG. WE JUST WANTED TO CONGRATULATE YOU FOR YOUR SUCCESS.
I'M GLAD THAT WE'VE GOT HALF OF THE EGGS LEFT, SO LET THE BATTLE CONTINUE.

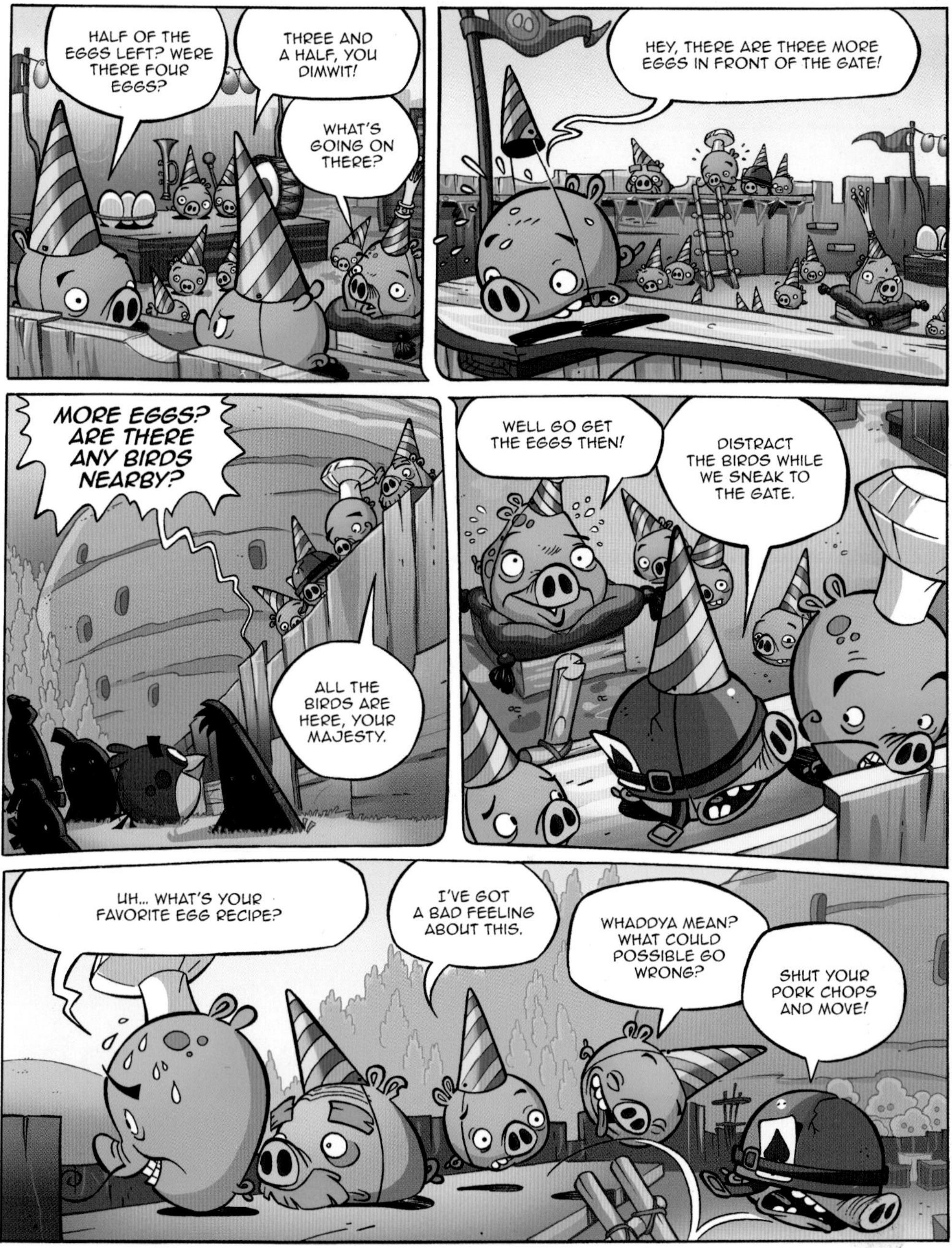
HALF OF THE EGGS LEFT? WERE THERE FOUR EGGS?
THREE AND A HALF, YOU DIMWIT!
WHAT'S GOING ON THERE?
HEY, THERE ARE THREE MORE EGGS IN FRONT OF THE GATE!
MORE EGGS? ARE THERE ANY BIRDS NEARBY?
ALL THE BIRDS ARE HERE, YOUR MAJESTY.
WELL GO GET THE EGGS THEN!
DISTRACT THE BIRDS WHILE WE SNEAK TO THE GATE.
UH... WHAT'S YOUR FAVORITE EGG RECIPE?
I'VE GOT A BAD FEELING ABOUT THIS.
WHADDYA MEAN? WHAT COULD POSSIBLE GO WRONG?
SHUT YOUR PORK CHOPS AND MOVE!

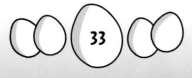

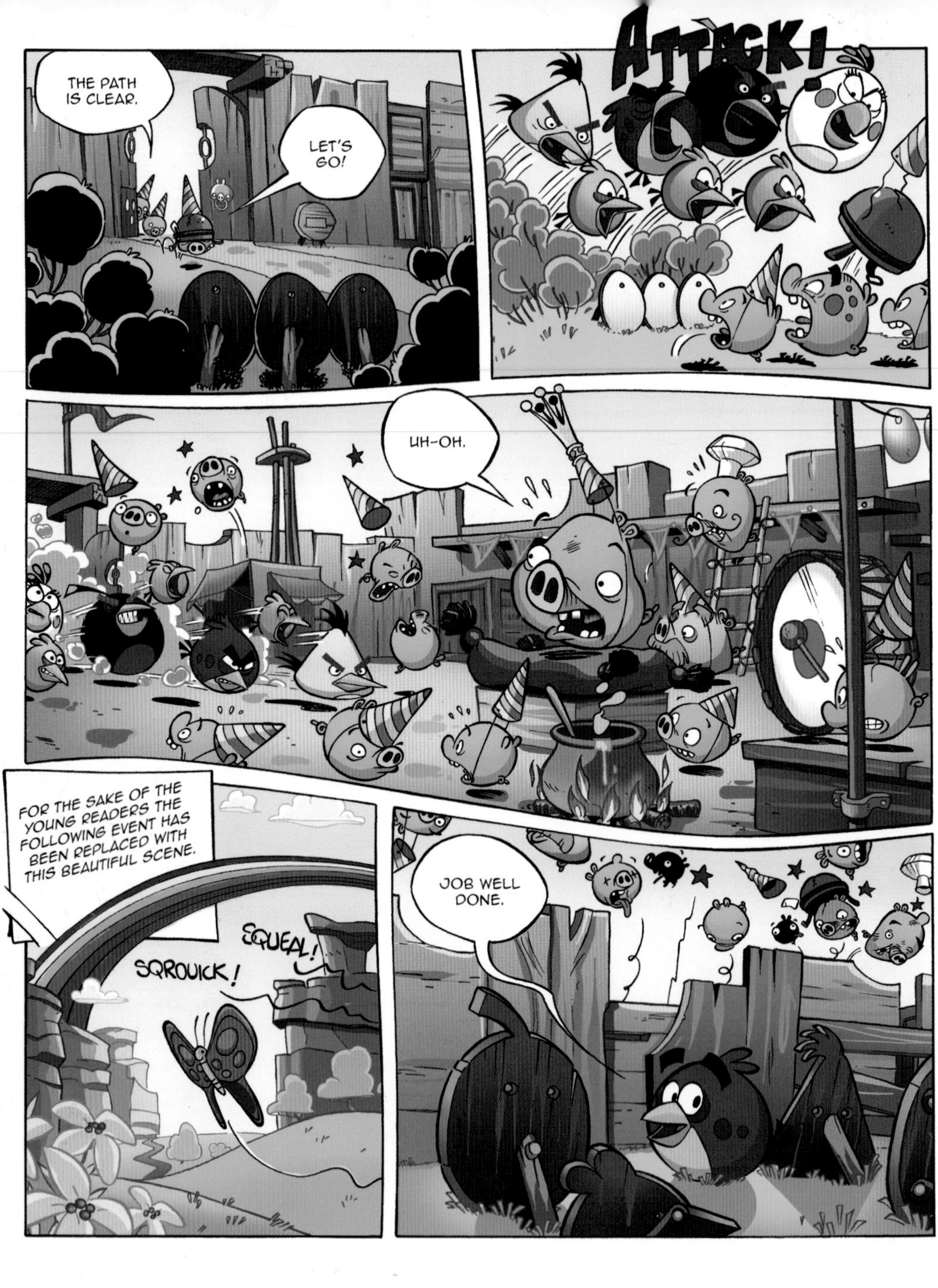
THE PATH IS CLEAR.
LET'S GO!
ATTACK!
UH-OH.
FOR THE SAKE OF THE YOUNG READERS THE FOLLOWING EVENT HAS BEEN REPLACED WITH THIS BEAUTIFUL SCENE.
SQROUICK!
SQUEAL!
JOB WELL DONE.

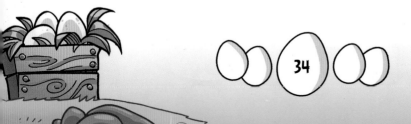

LATER:
WOULD YOU JOIN US FOR A PICNIC, BOYS?
SURE, CHUCK!
MUNCH! YOUR COOKING IS DELICIOUS, MATILDA!
AS ALWAYS!
THANK YOU, BOYS.
BUT... SHOULDN'T SOMEONE BE GUARDING THE EGGS?
I DON'T BELIEVE THAT WE HAVE TO WORRY ABOUT THAT FOR A WHILE.
DO YOU THINK THAT THEY ARE REAL?
I THINK THAT I DON'T WANT TO FIND OUT.
THE END

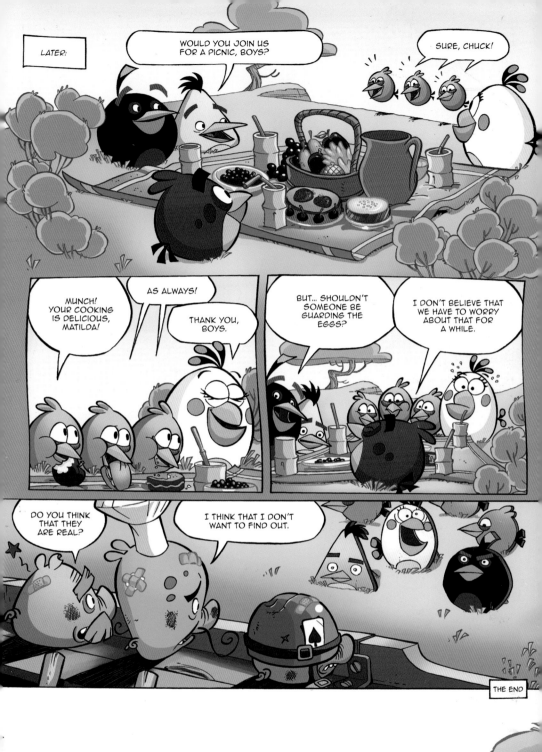

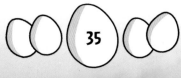

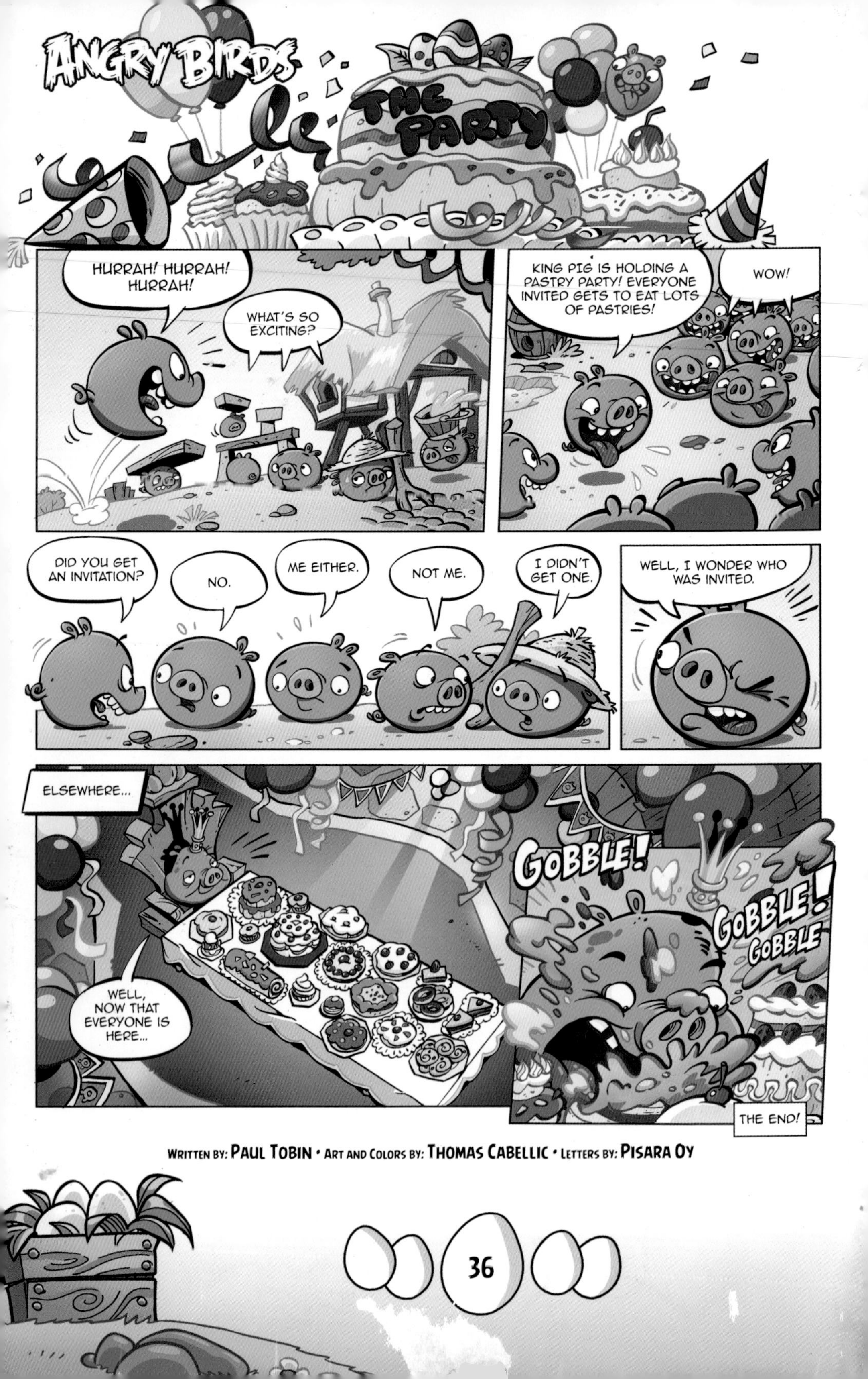
ANGRY BIRDS
THE PARTY
HURRAH! HURRAH! HURRAH!
WHAT'S SO EXCITING?
KING PIG IS HOLDING A PASTRY PARTY! EVERYONE INVITED GETS TO EAT LOTS OF PASTRIES!
WOW!
DID YOU GET AN INVITATION?
NO.
ME EITHER.
NOT ME.
I DIDN'T GET ONE.
WELL, I WONDER WHO WAS INVITED.
ELSEWHERE...
WELL, NOW THAT EVERYONE IS HERE...
GOBBLE!
GOBBLE!
GOBBLE
THE END!

Written by: Paul Tobin • Art and Colors by: Thomas Cabellic • Letters by: Pisara Oy

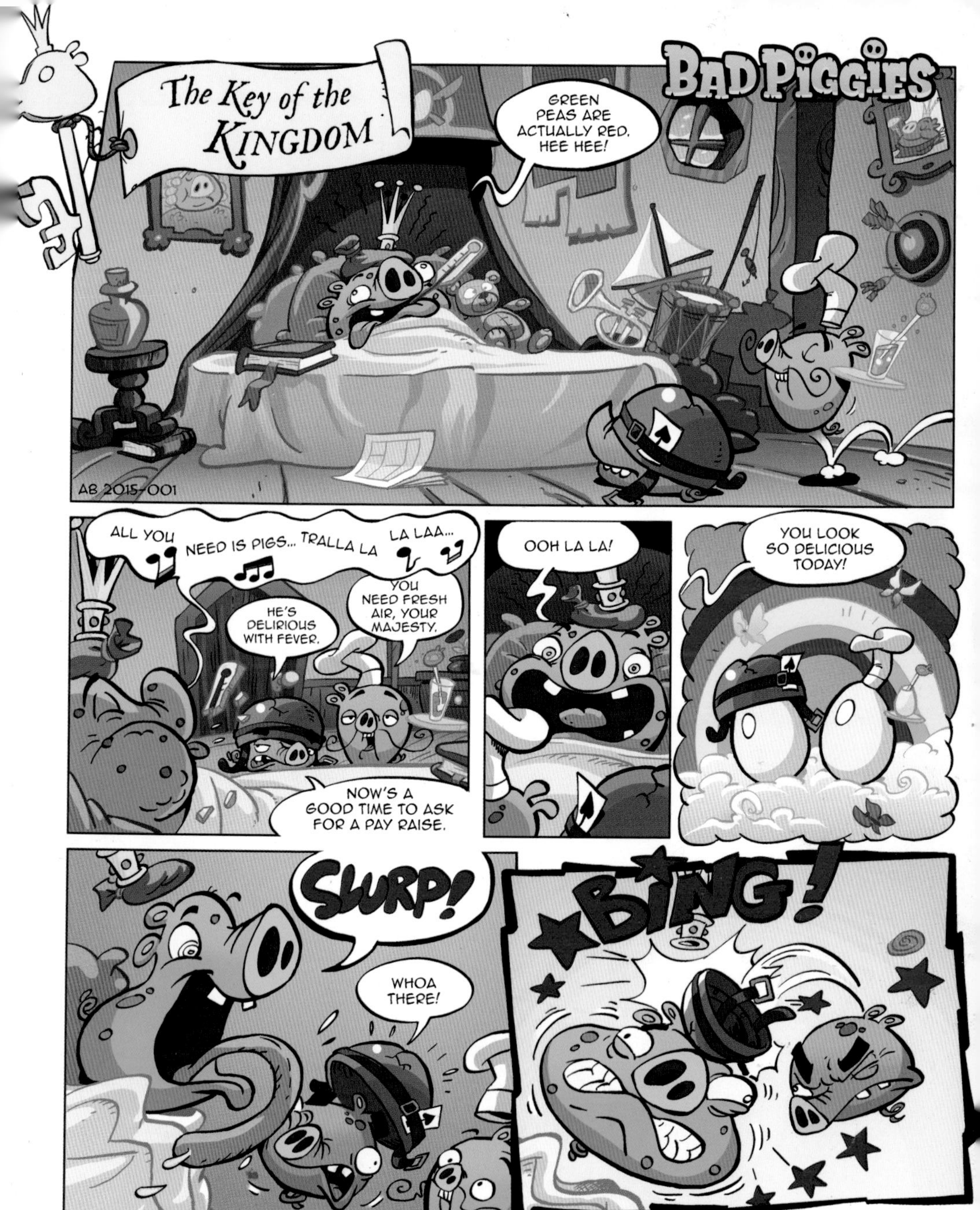

The Key of the KINGDOM
BAD PIGGIES
GREEN PEAS ARE ACTUALLY RED. HEE HEE!
AB 2015-001
ALL YOU NEED IS PIGS... TRALLA LA LA LAA...
HE'S DELIRIOUS WITH FEVER.
YOU NEED FRESH AIR, YOUR MAJESTY.
NOW'S A GOOD TIME TO ASK FOR A PAY RAISE.
OOH LA LA!
YOU LOOK SO DELICIOUS TODAY!
SLURP!
WHOA THERE!
BING!

WRITTEN BY: JULIAN FREY • ART BY: THOMAS CABELLIC • COLORS BY: DIGIKORE • LETTERS BY: PISARA OY

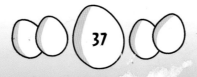

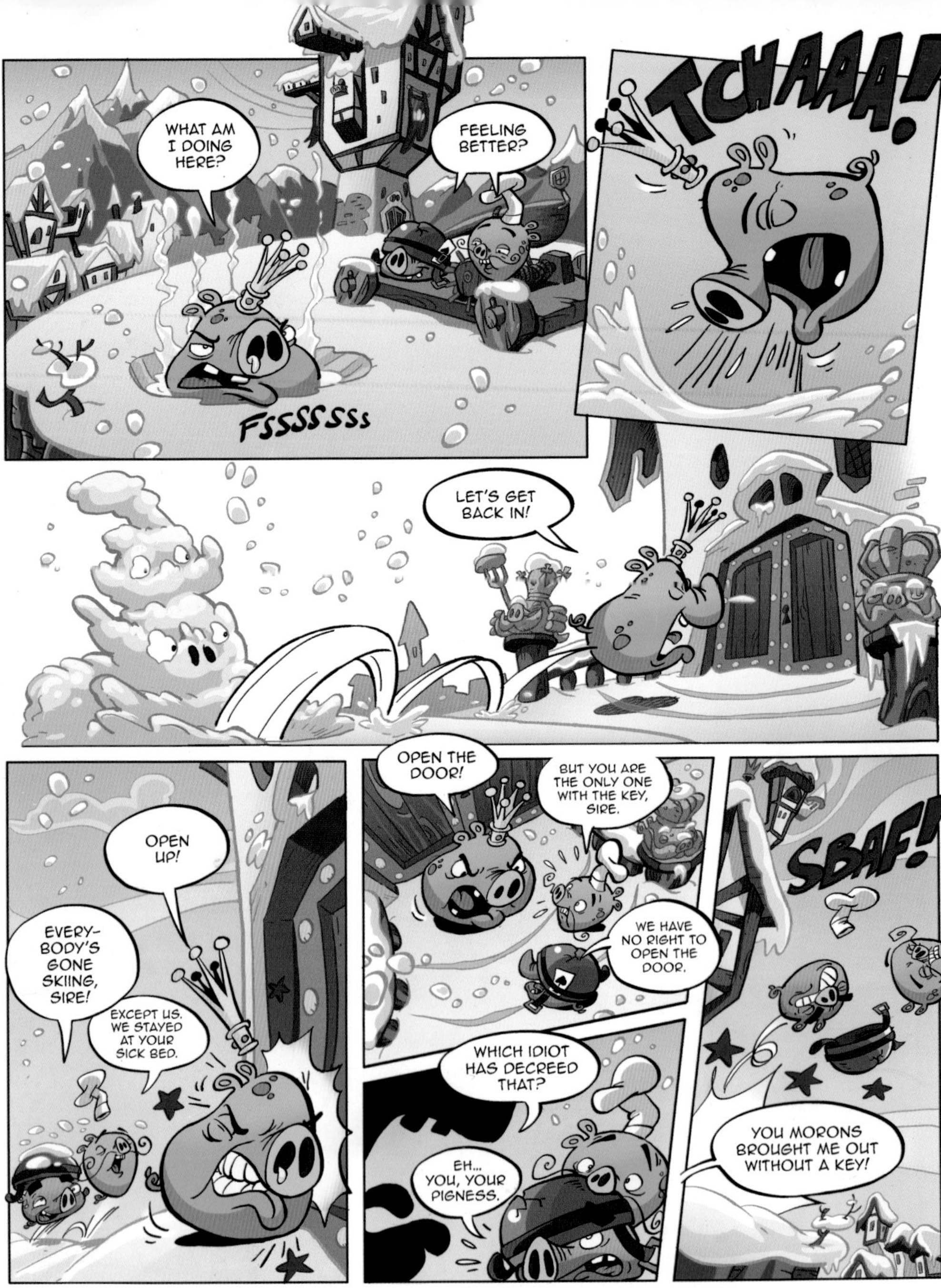
WHAT AM I DOING HERE?
FEELING BETTER?
FSSSSSSS
TCHAAA!
LET'S GET BACK IN!
OPEN UP!
EVERY-BODY'S GONE SKIING, SIRE!
EXCEPT US. WE STAYED AT YOUR SICK BED.
OPEN THE DOOR!
BUT YOU ARE THE ONLY ONE WITH THE KEY, SIRE.
WE HAVE NO RIGHT TO OPEN THE DOOR.
WHICH IDIOT HAS DECREED THAT?
EH... YOU, YOUR PIGNESS.
SBAF!
YOU MORONS BROUGHT ME OUT WITHOUT A KEY!

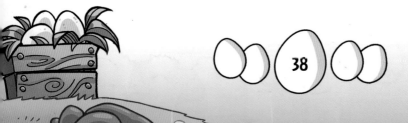

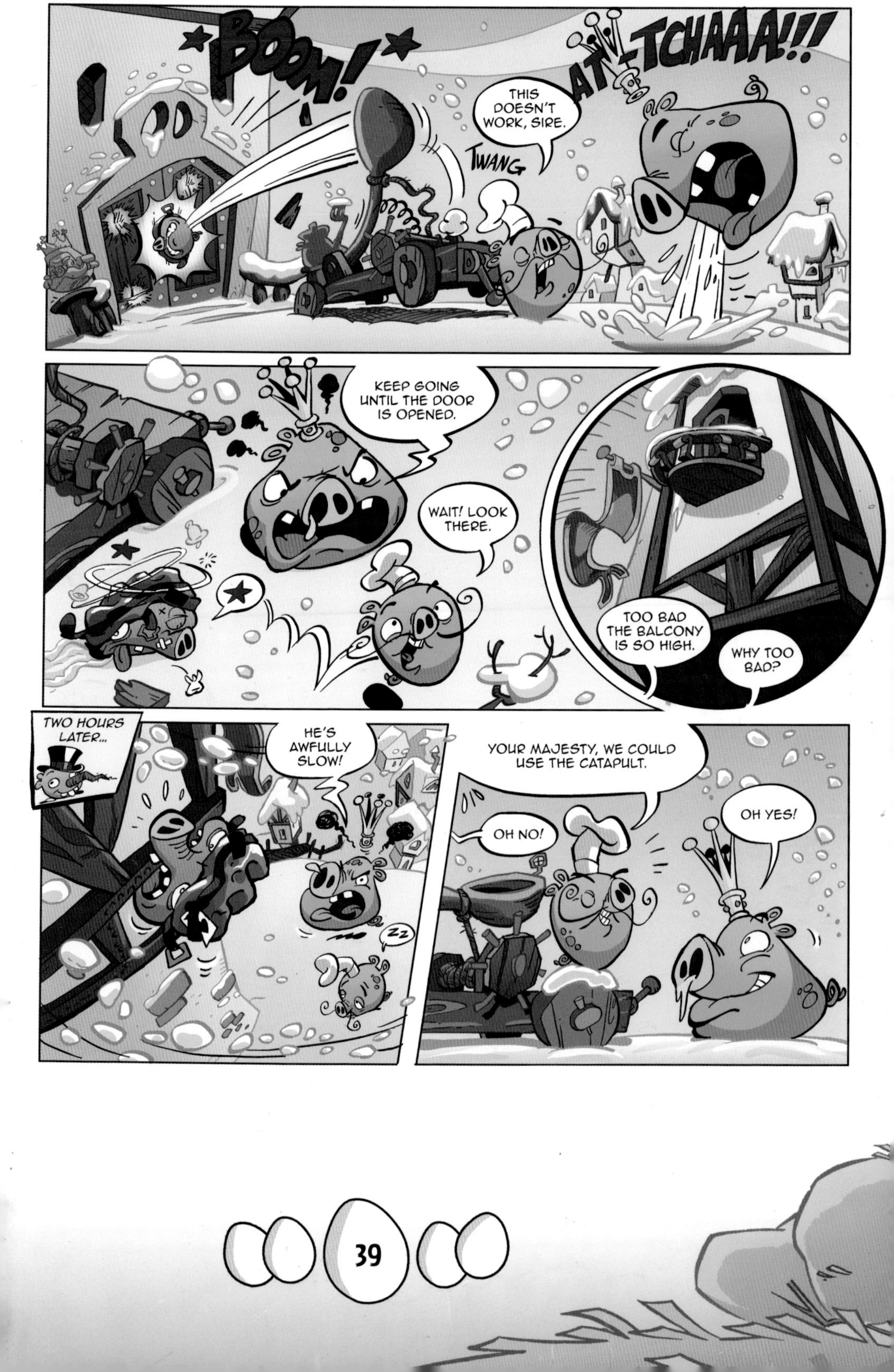
BOOM!
AT-TCHAAA!!!
THIS DOESN'T WORK, SIRE.
TWANG
KEEP GOING UNTIL THE DOOR IS OPENED.
WAIT! LOOK THERE.
TOO BAD THE BALCONY IS SO HIGH.
WHY TOO BAD?
TWO HOURS LATER...
HE'S AWFULLY SLOW!
YOUR MAJESTY, WE COULD USE THE CATAPULT.
OH NO!
OH YES!

OH NO!
OH YES!
YOU ONLY NEED TO ALIGN THE DOOHICKEY.
ATCHAAAAA
CLIC
WOAAAAAAAAAAAA!!!
BOING
TWANG!
I'M ALMOST THERE!

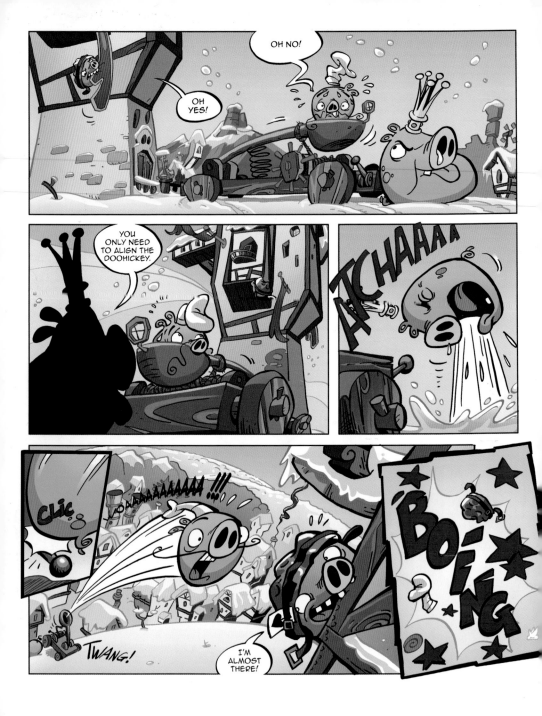

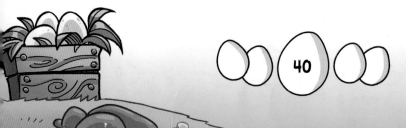

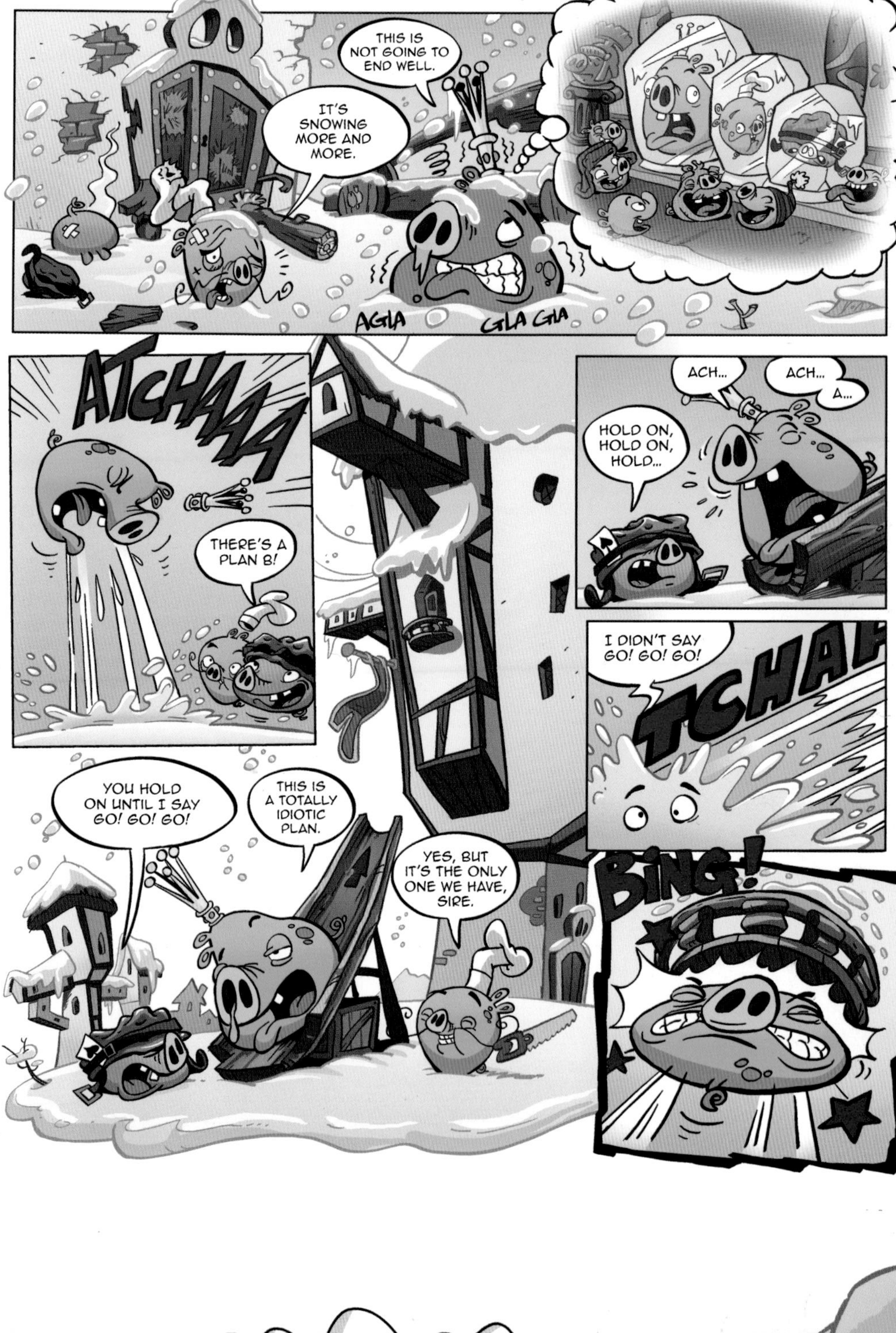
THIS IS NOT GOING TO END WELL.
IT'S SNOWING MORE AND MORE.
AGLA
GLA GLA
ATCHAAAA
THERE'S A PLAN B!
ACH...
ACH... A...
HOLD ON, HOLD ON, HOLD...
YOU HOLD ON UNTIL I SAY GO! GO! GO!
THIS IS A TOTALLY IDIOTIC PLAN.
YES, BUT IT'S THE ONLY ONE WE HAVE, SIRE.
I DIDN'T SAY GO! GO! GO!
TCHAA
BING!

GOT IT!
OH YES, I PUT IT IN MY CROWN SO I WOULDN'T LOSE IT! I'M A GENIUS!
UH-OH!
THE KEY!
SPROUT!
CRACKK
LOST IT.
YOU GANG OF BUNGLERS!
IT CAN'T BE FAR.
WE'LL FIND IT, SIRE.
THE END

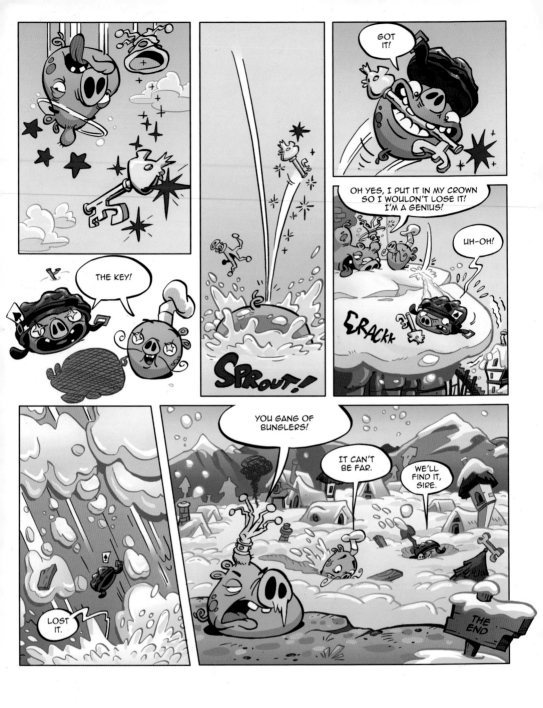

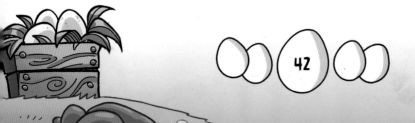

HAVE YE TRAVELED THE WORLD YET, READER?
MOST FOLKS FEEL PRETTY BIG UNTIL THEY GO ON A REAL JOURNEY, THEN REALIZE HOW SMALL THEY REALLY ARE. OUR TALE TODAY IS OF A YOUNG BIRD WHO FELT BOTH WAYS!
THIS YOUNG DOCTOR TOLD ME HOW HE FOUND HIMSELF ON AN OCEAN VOYAGE AT A VERY STORMY TIME IN THE SOUTH SEAS! HIS NAME: GULLIBIRD. AND THESE FANTASTIC JOURNALS DESCRIBE...
GULLIBIRD'S TRAVELS
TAKE IN THE SAILS!
SHIP'S SURGEON REPORTING FOR DUTY!
ANGRY BIRDS™
BATTEN DOWN THE HATCHES!
DOES ANYONE NEED A BANDAGE, PERHAPS? A SPLINTER I CAN REMOVE?
IF YE CAN REMOVE THAT ROCK WE'RE ABOUT TO RUN UPON, THAT WOULD BE GREAT!
YAWK!
KEE-RAASHH
AB 2013-087

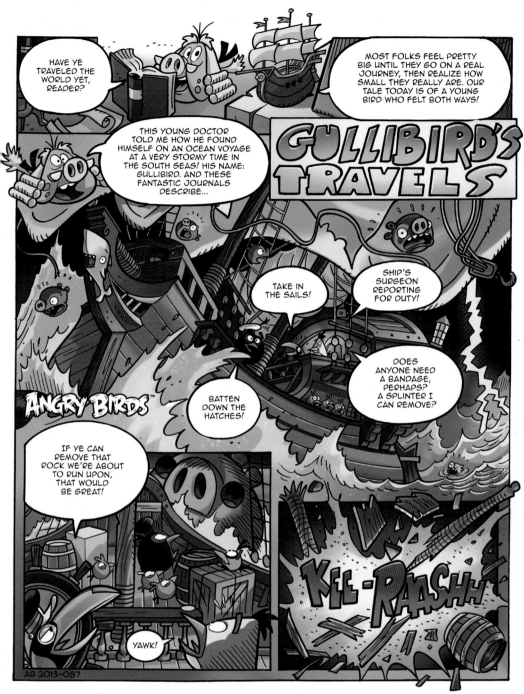

WRITTEN BY: PAUL TOBIN • ART BY: MARCO GERVASIO • COLORS BY: NICOLA PASQUETTO • LETTERS BY: PISARA OY

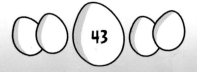

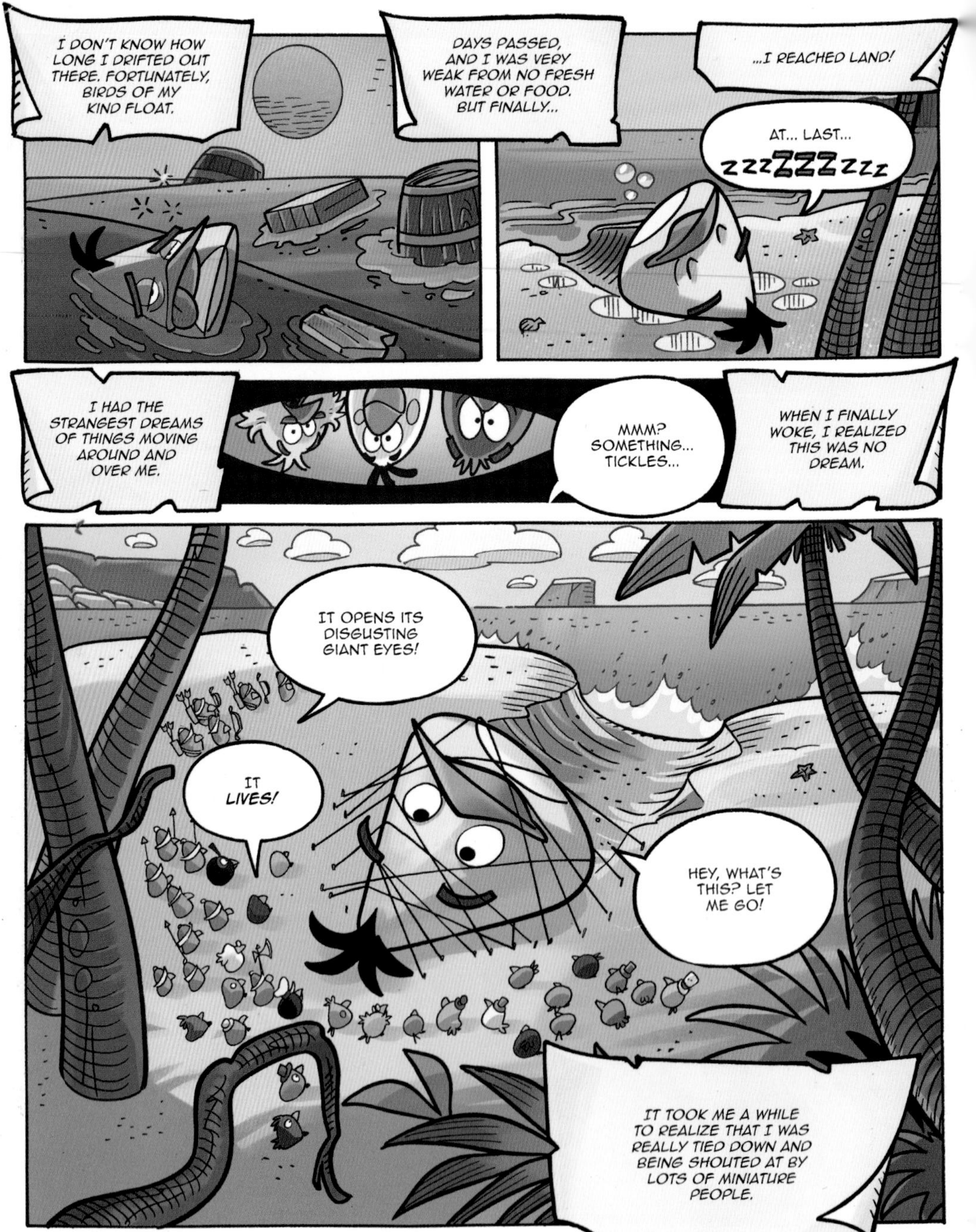
I DON'T KNOW HOW LONG I DRIFTED OUT THERE. FORTUNATELY, BIRDS OF MY KIND FLOAT.
DAYS PASSED, AND I WAS VERY WEAK FROM NO FRESH WATER OR FOOD. BUT FINALLY...
...I REACHED LAND!
AT... LAST... zzzZZZzzz
I HAD THE STRANGEST DREAMS OF THINGS MOVING AROUND AND OVER ME.
MMM? SOMETHING... TICKLES...
WHEN I FINALLY WOKE, I REALIZED THIS WAS NO DREAM.
IT OPENS ITS DISGUSTING GIANT EYES!
IT LIVES!
HEY, WHAT'S THIS? LET ME GO!
IT TOOK ME A WHILE TO REALIZE THAT I WAS REALLY TIED DOWN AND BEING SHOUTED AT BY LOTS OF MINIATURE PEOPLE.

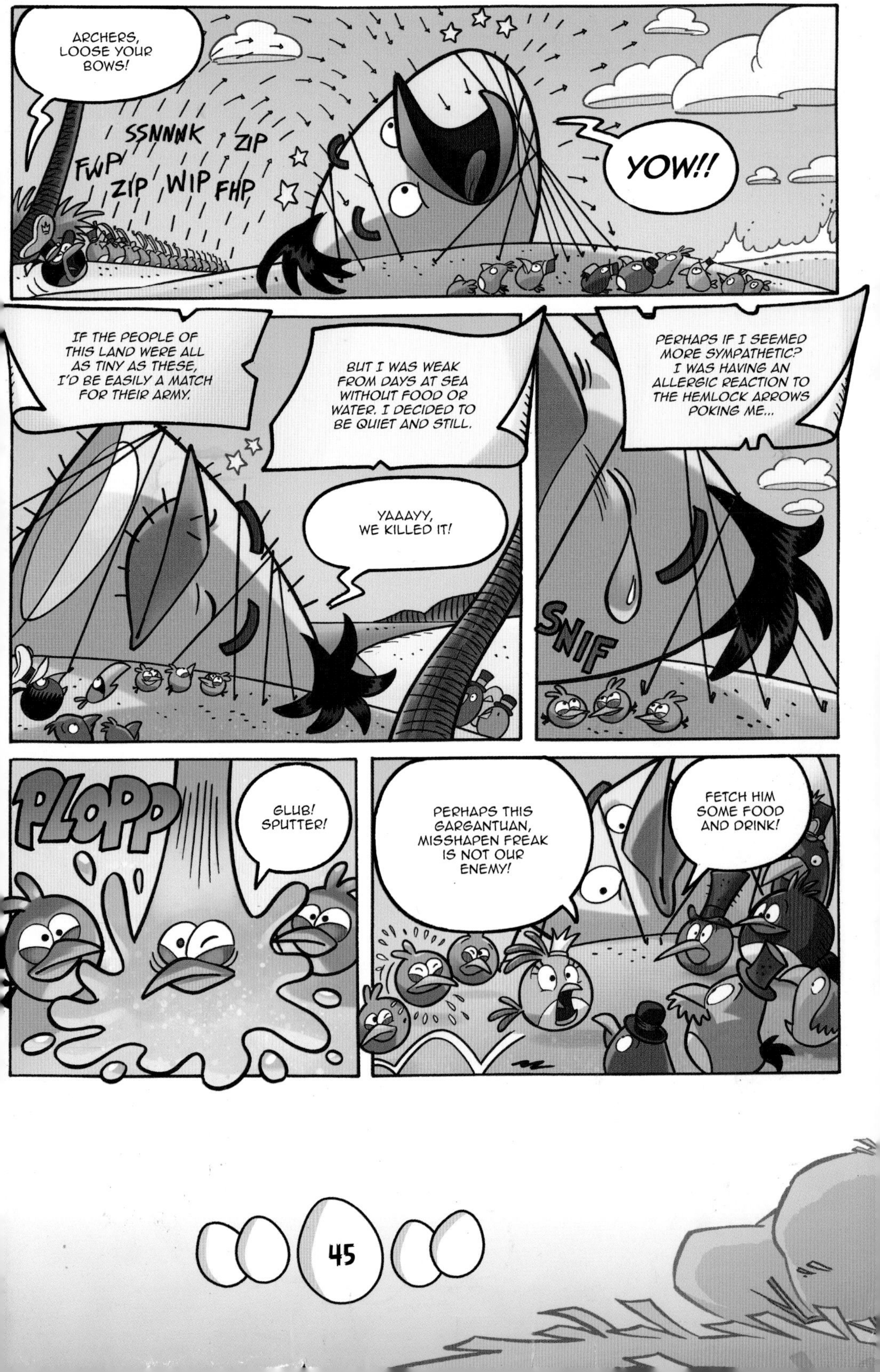
ARCHERS, LOOSE YOUR BOWS!
SSNNNK
ZIP
FWP
ZIP
WIP
FHP
YOW!!
IF THE PEOPLE OF THIS LAND WERE ALL AS TINY AS THESE, I'D BE EASILY A MATCH FOR THEIR ARMY.
BUT I WAS WEAK FROM DAYS AT SEA WITHOUT FOOD OR WATER. I DECIDED TO BE QUIET AND STILL.
YAAAYY, WE KILLED IT!
PERHAPS IF I SEEMED MORE SYMPATHETIC? I WAS HAVING AN ALLERGIC REACTION TO THE HEMLOCK ARROWS POKING ME...
SNIF
PLOPP
GLUB! SPUTTER!
PERHAPS THIS GARGANTUAN, MISSHAPEN FREAK IS NOT OUR ENEMY!
FETCH HIM SOME FOOD AND DRINK!

THESE WEE PEOPLE WERE EXCEPTIONAL AT ENGINEERING. IN NO TIME THEY HAD BUILT...

...DEVICES CAPABLE OF FEEDING ME AND SOLVING MY THIRST.

HURRHGH!!!

GLUBFH!

- AND MY REST.

ZZZZ

AWWK

ARE YOU SURE WE DIDN'T KILL HIM?

WHEN I WOKE THEY HAD BUILT AN ENORMOUS CART TO TAKE ME TO THEIR PALACE.

JUST FYI, I CAN ACTUALLY MOVE AROUND AND DO THINGS FOR MYSELF, LITTLE PEOPLE.

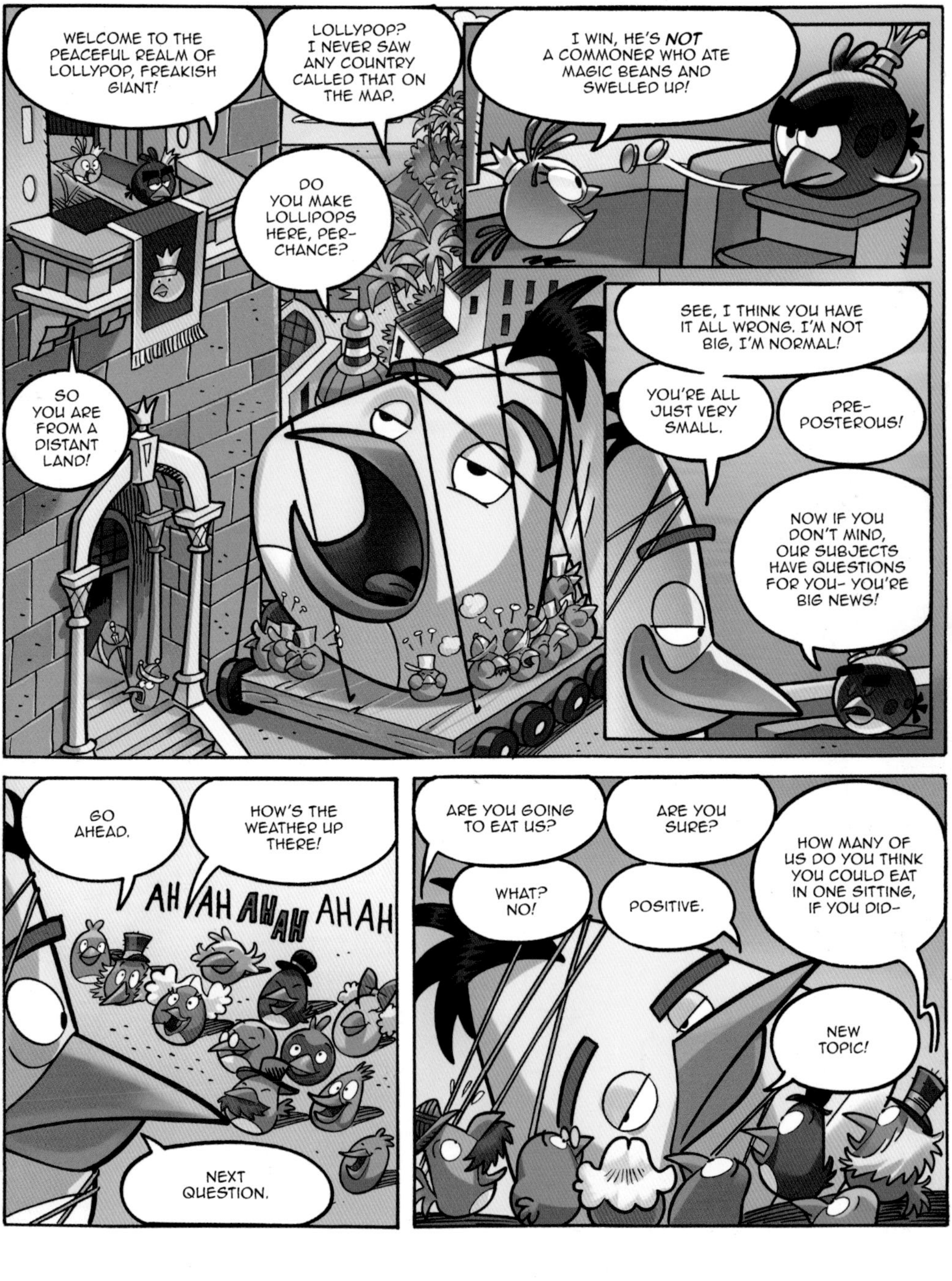
WELCOME TO THE PEACEFUL REALM OF LOLLYPOP, FREAKISH GIANT!
LOLLYPOP? I NEVER SAW ANY COUNTRY CALLED THAT ON THE MAP.
SO YOU ARE FROM A DISTANT LAND!
DO YOU MAKE LOLLIPOPS HERE, PER-CHANCE?
I WIN, HE'S **NOT** A COMMONER WHO ATE MAGIC BEANS AND SWELLED UP!
SEE, I THINK YOU HAVE IT ALL WRONG. I'M NOT BIG, I'M NORMAL!
YOU'RE ALL JUST VERY SMALL.
PRE-POSTEROUS!
NOW IF YOU DON'T MIND, OUR SUBJECTS HAVE QUESTIONS FOR YOU- YOU'RE BIG NEWS!
GO AHEAD.
HOW'S THE WEATHER UP THERE!
AH AH AHAH AHAH
NEXT QUESTION.
ARE YOU GOING TO EAT US?
WHAT? NO!
ARE YOU SURE?
POSITIVE.
HOW MANY OF US DO YOU THINK YOU COULD EAT IN ONE SITTING, IF YOU DID-
NEW TOPIC!

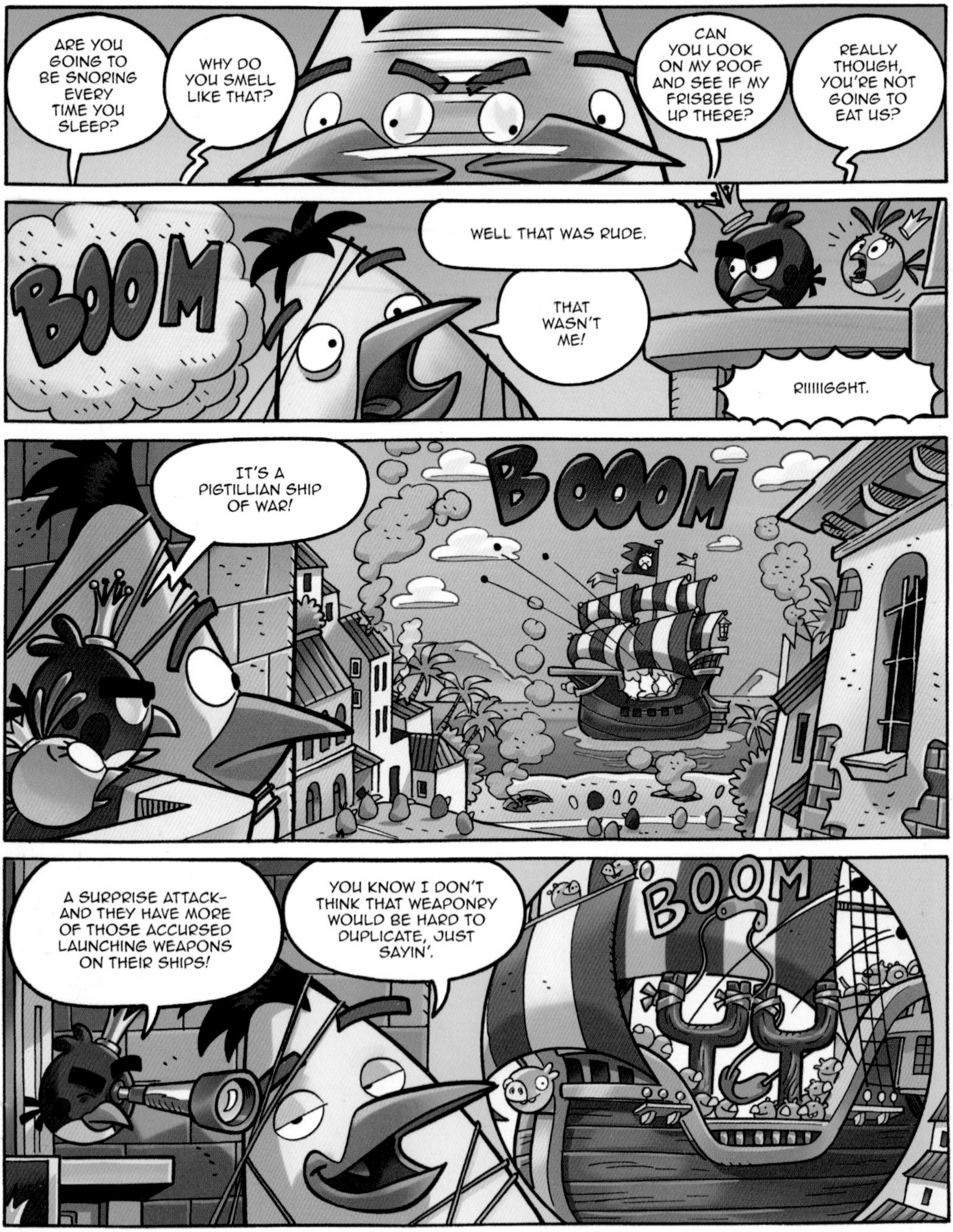
ARE YOU GOING TO BE SNORING EVERY TIME YOU SLEEP?
WHY DO YOU SMELL LIKE THAT?
CAN YOU LOOK ON MY ROOF AND SEE IF MY FRISBEE IS UP THERE?
REALLY THOUGH, YOU'RE NOT GOING TO EAT US?
BOOM
WELL THAT WAS RUDE.
THAT WASN'T ME!
RIIIIIGGHT.
IT'S A PIGTILLIAN SHIP OF WAR!
BOOOM
A SURPRISE ATTACK– AND THEY HAVE MORE OF THOSE ACCURSED LAUNCHING WEAPONS ON THEIR SHIPS!
YOU KNOW I DON'T THINK THAT WEAPONRY WOULD BE HARD TO DUPLICATE, JUST SAYIN'.
BOOM

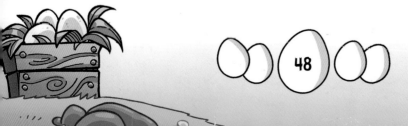

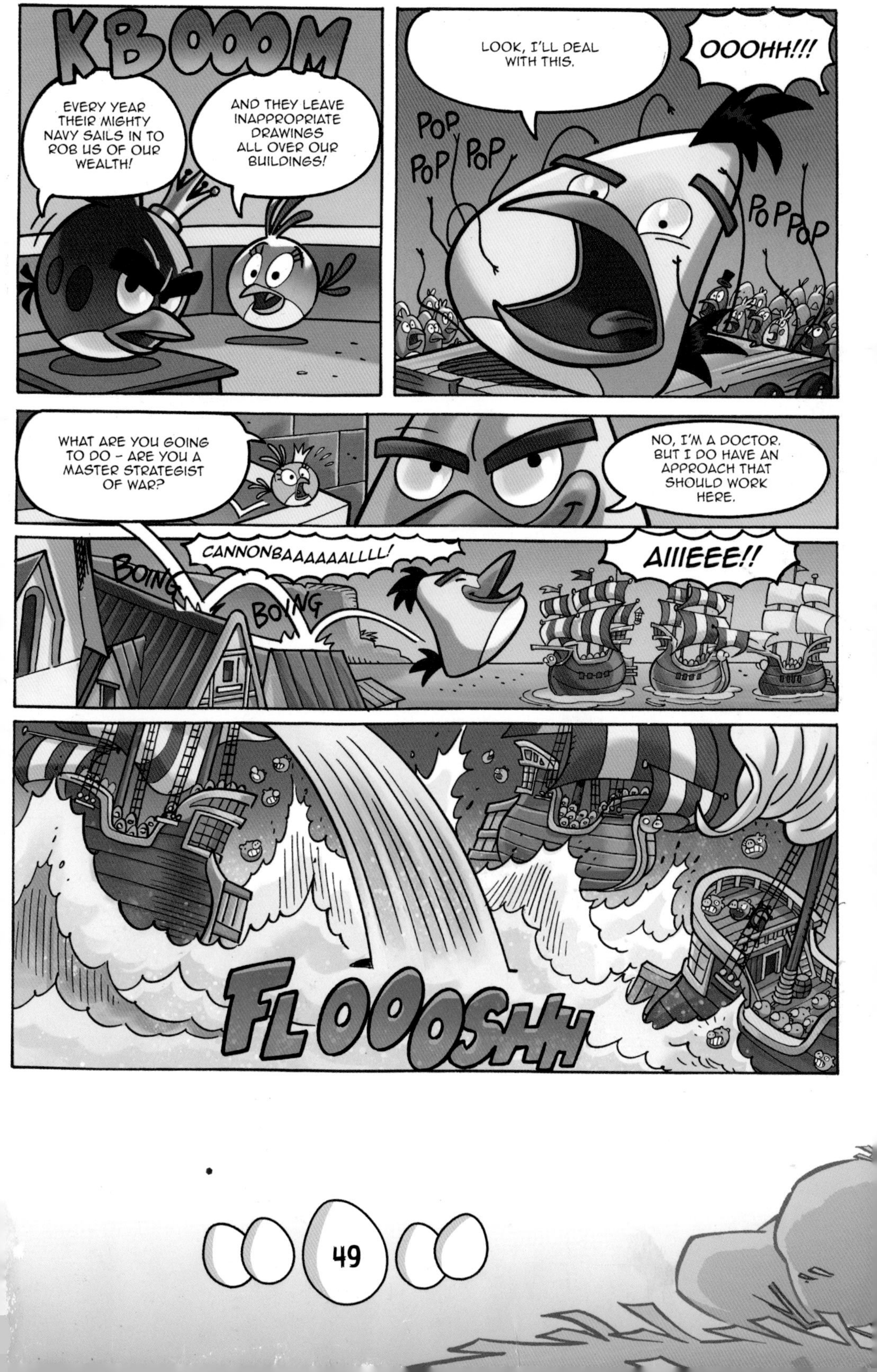
KBOOOM
EVERY YEAR THEIR MIGHTY NAVY SAILS IN TO ROB US OF OUR WEALTH!
AND THEY LEAVE INAPPROPRIATE DRAWINGS ALL OVER OUR BUILDINGS!
LOOK, I'LL DEAL WITH THIS.
OOOHH!!!
POP POP POP
POPPOP
WHAT ARE YOU GOING TO DO - ARE YOU A MASTER STRATEGIST OF WAR?
NO, I'M A DOCTOR. BUT I DO HAVE AN APPROACH THAT SHOULD WORK HERE.
CANNONBAAAAAALLLL!
AIIIEEE!!
BOING
BOING
FLOOOSHH

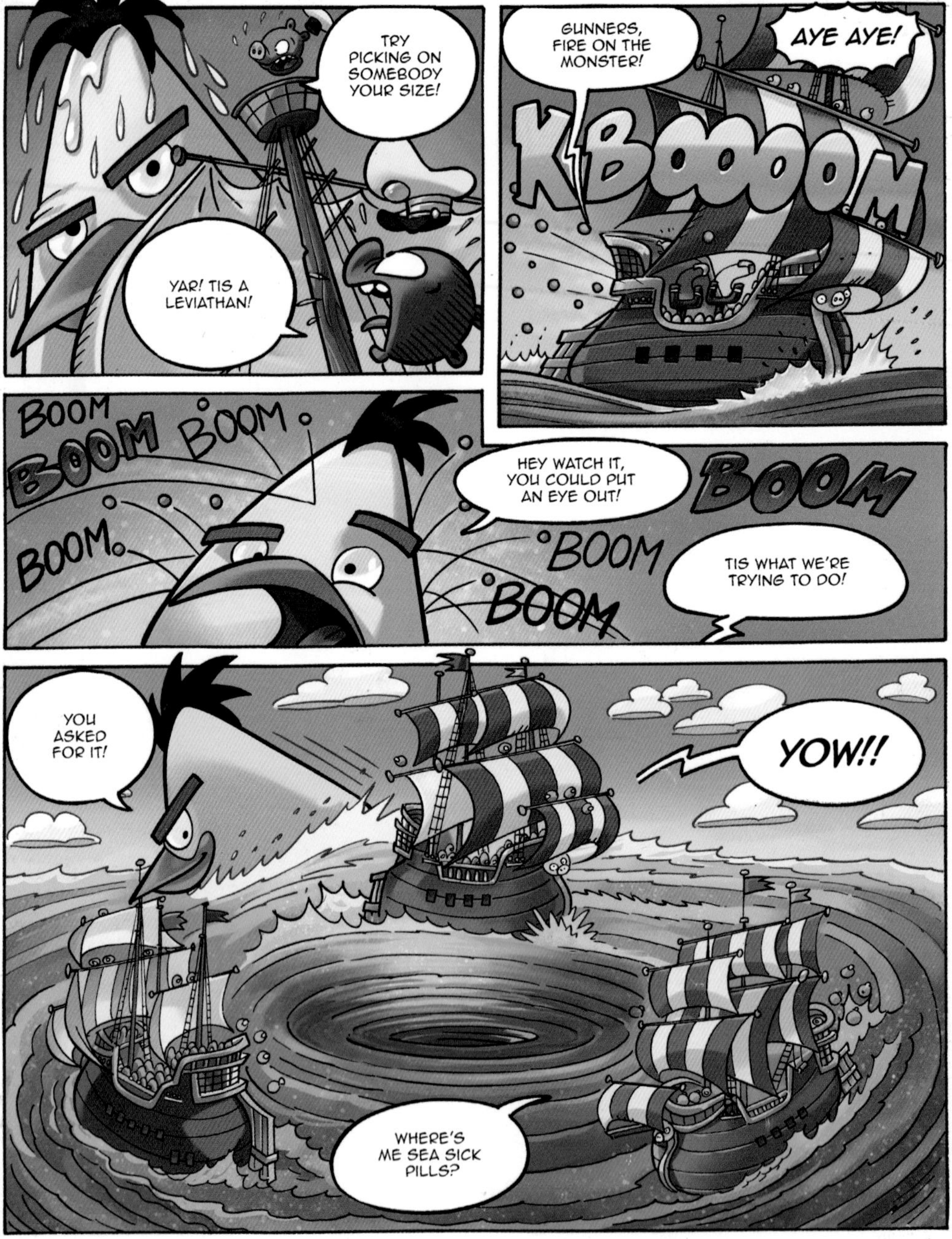
TRY PICKING ON SOMEBODY YOUR SIZE!
YAR! TIS A LEVIATHAN!
GUNNERS, FIRE ON THE MONSTER!
AYE AYE!
KBOOOOM
BOOM
BOOM
BOOM
BOOM
HEY WATCH IT, YOU COULD PUT AN EYE OUT!
BOOM
BOOM
BOOM
TIS WHAT WE'RE TRYING TO DO!
YOU ASKED FOR IT!
YOW!!
WHERE'S ME SEA SICK PILLS?

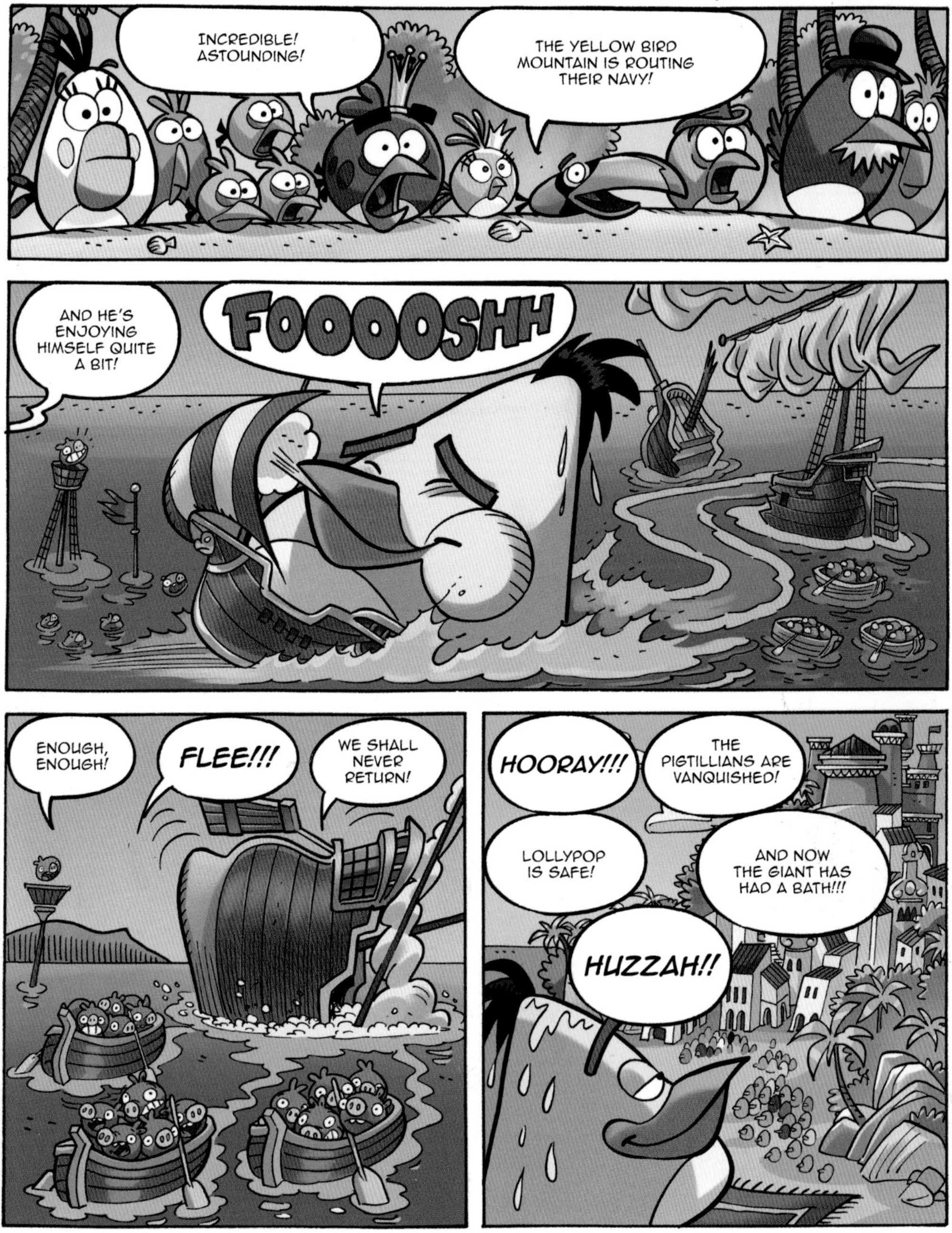
INCREDIBLE! ASTOUNDING!
THE YELLOW BIRD MOUNTAIN IS ROUTING THEIR NAVY!
AND HE'S ENJOYING HIMSELF QUITE A BIT!
FOOOOSHH
ENOUGH, ENOUGH!
FLEE!!!
WE SHALL NEVER RETURN!
HOORAY!!!
THE PIGTILLIANS ARE VANQUISHED!
LOLLYPOP IS SAFE!
AND NOW THE GIANT HAS HAD A BATH!!!
HUZZAH!!

THE TINY FOLK OF LOLLYPOP CELEBRATED ALL DAY AND NIGHT, AND REWARDED ME CONSTANTLY.
I COULD GET USED TO THIS.
MORE CHOCOLATE MILK FOR THE GIANT!
GLUB GLU
BLOB BLUB
A TOAST TO OUR GARGANTUAN NEW FRIEND!
WHO, WHEN HE ARRIVED, SEEMED LIKE THE WORST THING TO EVER HAPPEN TO LOLLYPOP.
BUT IS REALLY, THE BEST!
HOOORRAY!!
YOU TINY FOLKS ARE THE BES-
BUUURRRPPPP!!
I ASSUME IN YOUR LAND THAT IS A TERM OF FRIENDSHIP.
GOOD NIGHT, VAST ONE.
IN THE MORNING WE SHALL TAKE YOU ON A SPECIAL TRIP.
OH BOY!
I WILL ADMIT I ENJOYED MY NEWFOUND RESPECT FROM THE PEOPLE OF THIS LAND.
EXCEPT FOR NOT HAVING SOMEWHERE COMFORTABLE TO SLEEP, I FELT I WAS STARTING TO FIT IN!

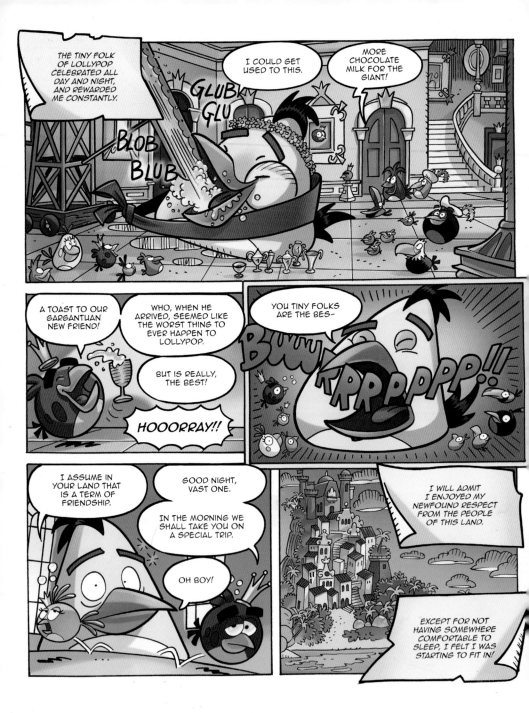

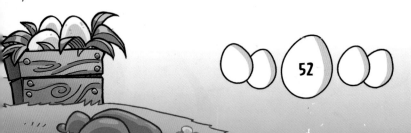

THIS IS A NICE TRADITION, GOING ON MORNING HIKES WITH YOUR PEOPLE.
YES, THIS WILL BE GOOD... EXERCISE- FOR YOU, GULLIBIRD!
WHAT DO YOU CALL THIS AREA?
WE CALL IT... PIGTILLIA!
AAAHH!! THE MONSTER HAS FOUND US!
IT WORKS FOR THE LILIPUTIANS!
NO STOMP ME!
GO FORTH MEN - WITH THE GIANT, WE CAN'T LOSE!
AS BEFORE, GULLIBIRD - CRUSH THEM! THE CITY IS OURS!
WHAT? NO, I WAS PROTECTING YOU BEFORE!
I'M NOT YOUR SECRET WEAPON! I THOUGHT YOU WERE A PEACEFUL LOT!
WE ARE, WHEN WE'RE LOSING!
SWISH

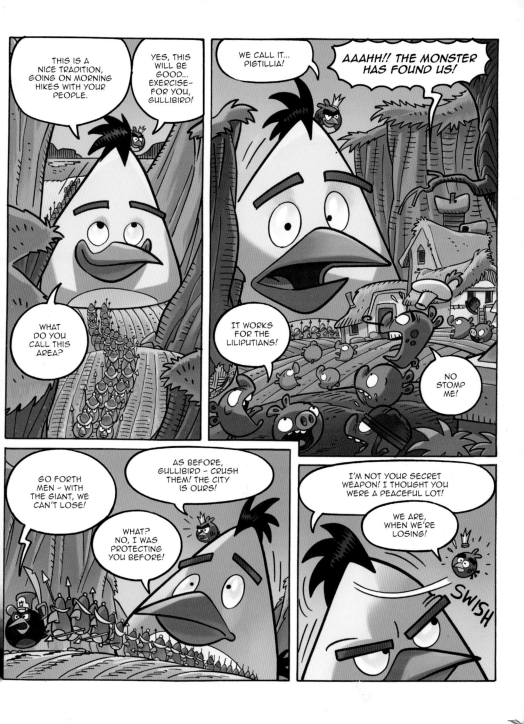

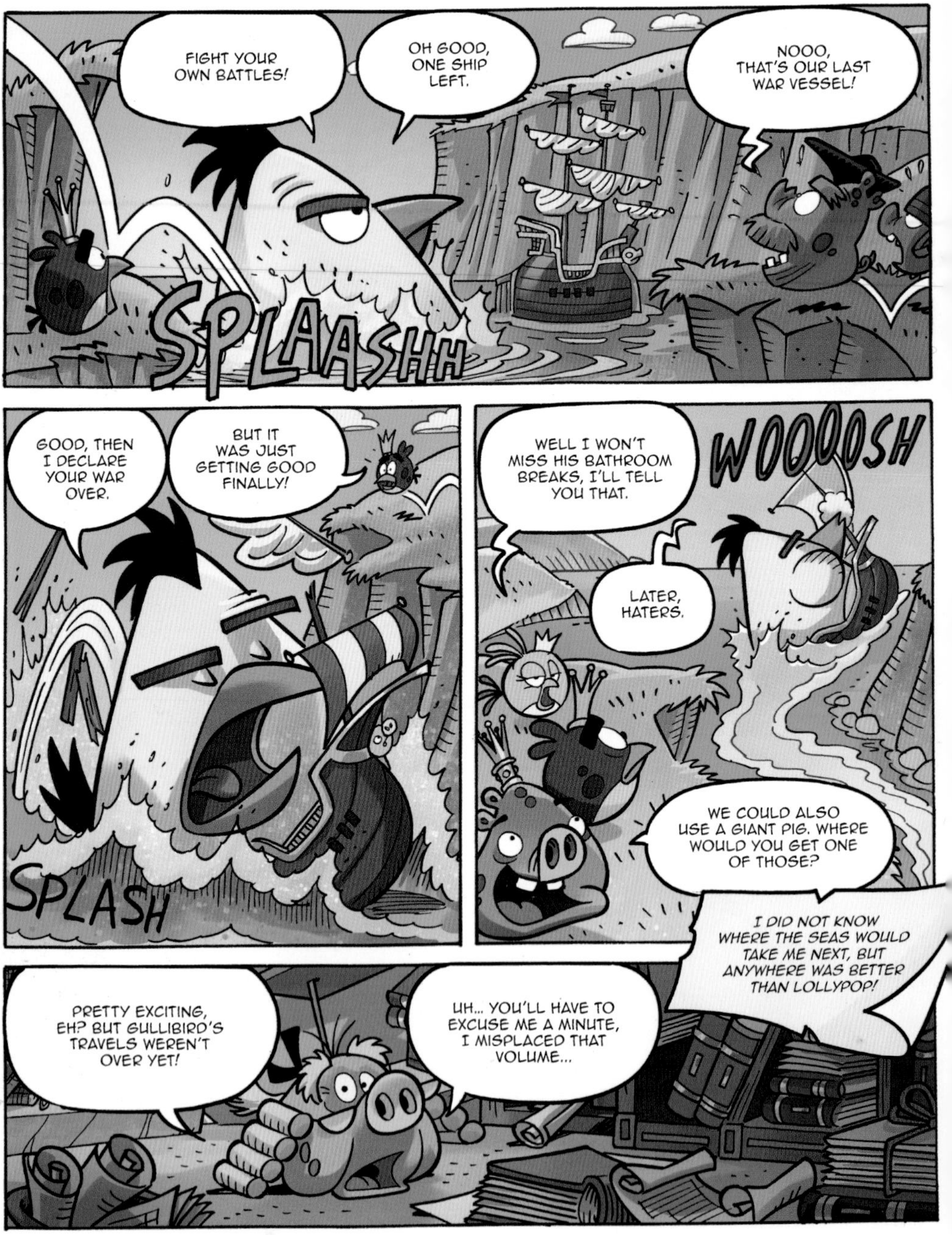
FIGHT YOUR OWN BATTLES!
OH GOOD, ONE SHIP LEFT.
NOOO, THAT'S OUR LAST WAR VESSEL!
SPLAASHH
GOOD, THEN I DECLARE YOUR WAR OVER.
BUT IT WAS JUST GETTING GOOD FINALLY!
SPLASH
WELL I WON'T MISS HIS BATHROOM BREAKS, I'LL TELL YOU THAT.
WOOOOSH
LATER, HATERS.
WE COULD ALSO USE A GIANT PIG. WHERE WOULD YOU GET ONE OF THOSE?
I DID NOT KNOW WHERE THE SEAS WOULD TAKE ME NEXT, BUT ANYWHERE WAS BETTER THAN LOLLYPOP!
PRETTY EXCITING, EH? BUT GULLIBIRD'S TRAVELS WEREN'T OVER YET!
UH... YOU'LL HAVE TO EXCUSE ME A MINUTE, I MISPLACED THAT VOLUME...

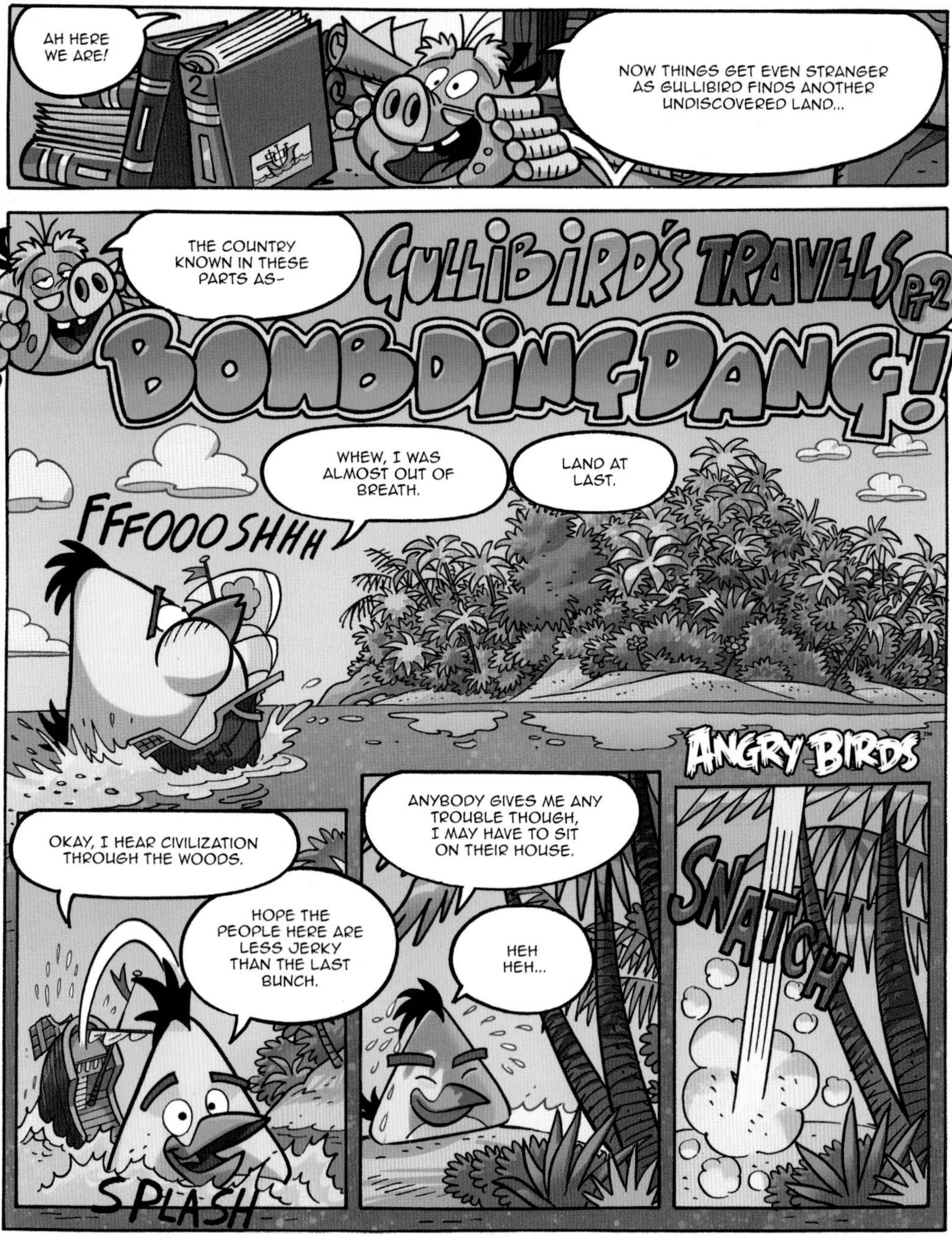
AH HERE WE ARE!
NOW THINGS GET EVEN STRANGER AS GULLIBIRD FINDS ANOTHER UNDISCOVERED LAND...
THE COUNTRY KNOWN IN THESE PARTS AS-
GULLIBIRD'S TRAVELS PT 2:
BOMBDINGDANG!
WHEW, I WAS ALMOST OUT OF BREATH.
LAND AT LAST.
FFFOOOSHHH
ANGRY BIRDS
OKAY, I HEAR CIVILIZATION THROUGH THE WOODS.
HOPE THE PEOPLE HERE ARE LESS JERKY THAN THE LAST BUNCH.
SPLASH
ANYBODY GIVES ME ANY TROUBLE THOUGH, I MAY HAVE TO SIT ON THEIR HOUSE.
HEH HEH...
SNATCH

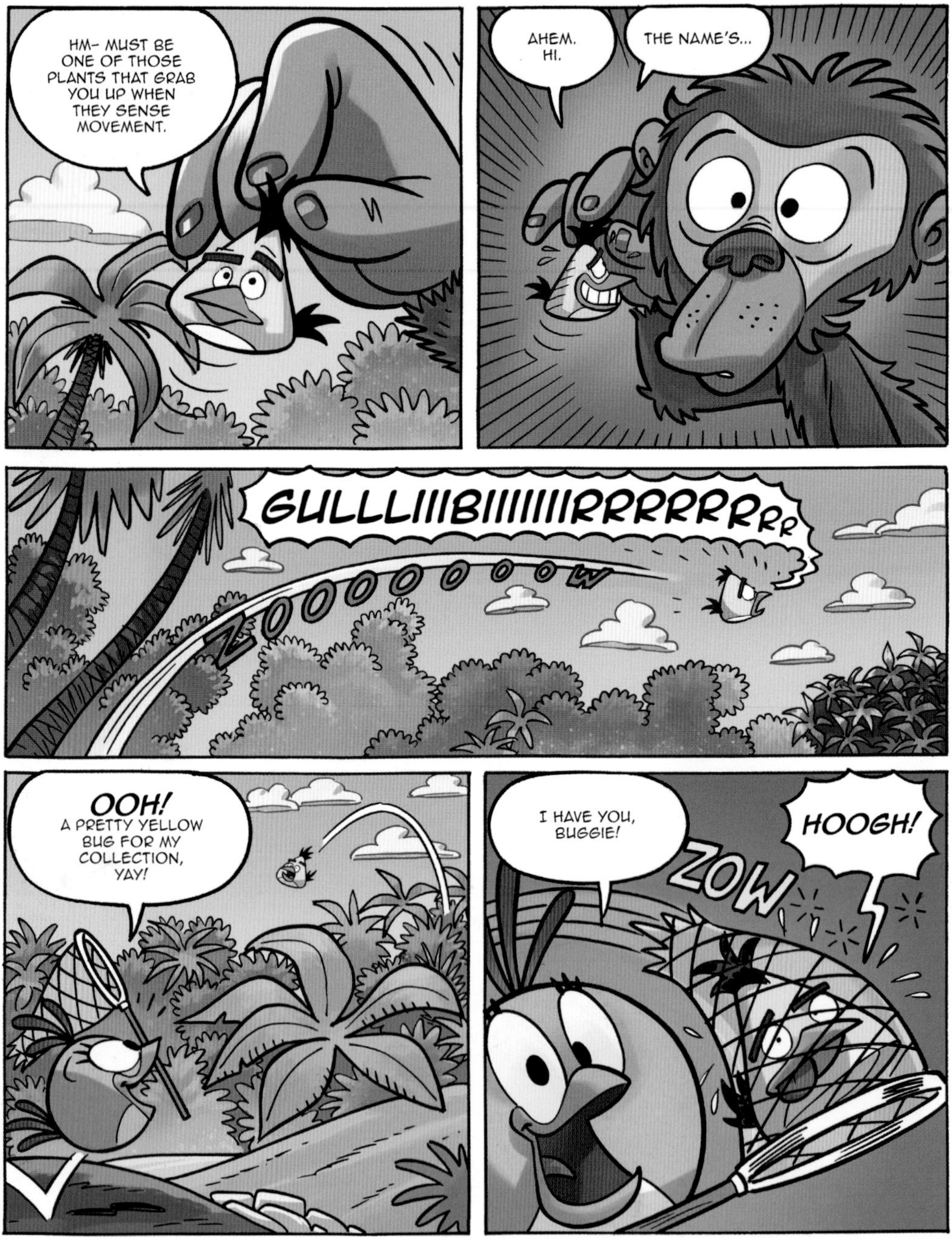

HM- MUST BE ONE OF THOSE PLANTS THAT GRAB YOU UP WHEN THEY SENSE MOVEMENT.
AHEM. HI.
THE NAME'S...
GULLLIIIIBIIIIIIIIRRRRRRRRR
ZOOOOOOOOOW
OOH! A PRETTY YELLOW BUG FOR MY COLLECTION, YAY!
I HAVE YOU, BUGGIE!
ZOW
HOOGH!

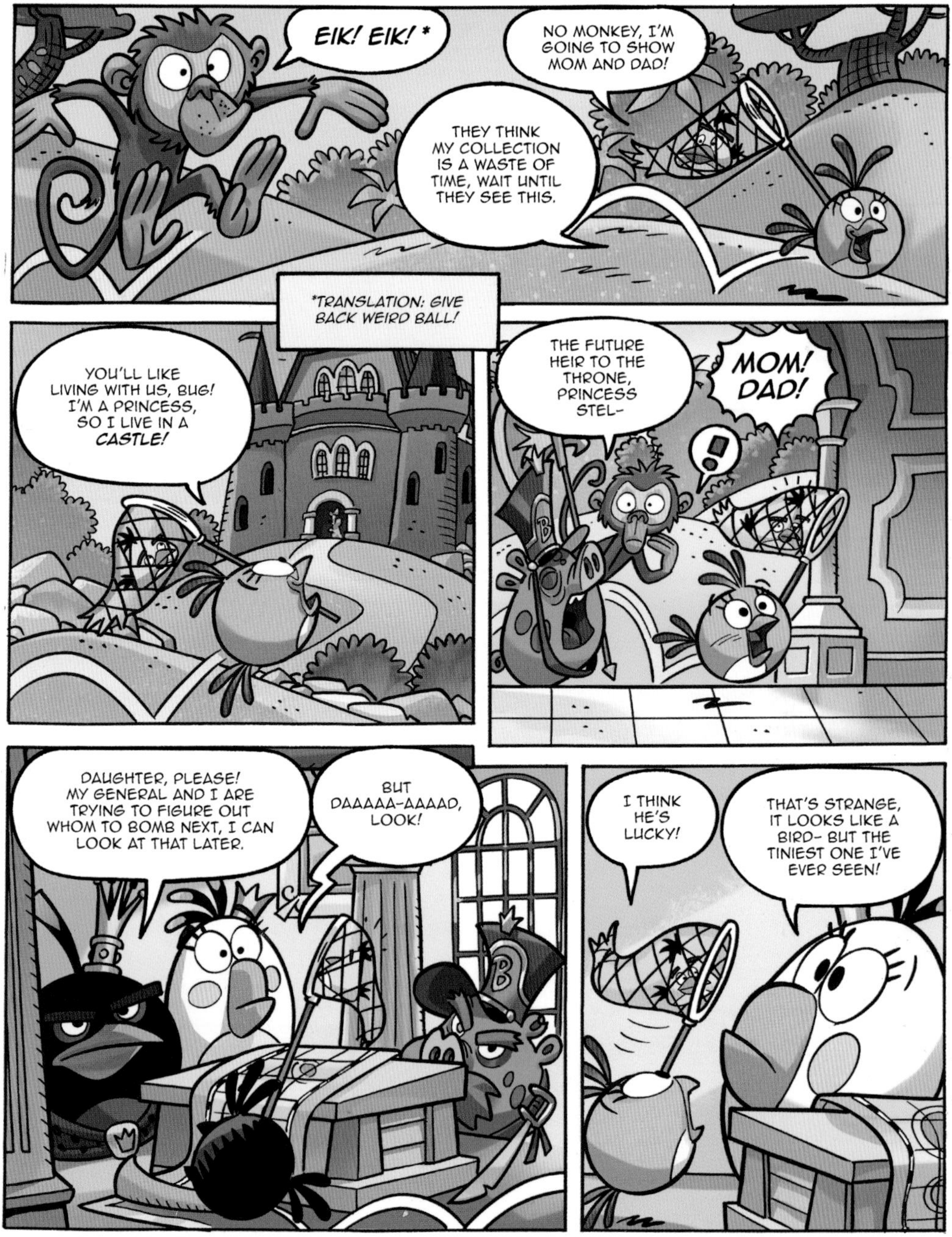
EIK! EIK! *
NO MONKEY, I'M GOING TO SHOW MOM AND DAD!
THEY THINK MY COLLECTION IS A WASTE OF TIME, WAIT UNTIL THEY SEE THIS.
*TRANSLATION: GIVE BACK WEIRD BALL!
YOU'LL LIKE LIVING WITH US, BUG! I'M A PRINCESS, SO I LIVE IN A CASTLE!
THE FUTURE HEIR TO THE THRONE, PRINCESS STEL-
MOM! DAD!
!
DAUGHTER, PLEASE! MY GENERAL AND I ARE TRYING TO FIGURE OUT WHOM TO BOMB NEXT, I CAN LOOK AT THAT LATER.
BUT DAAAAA-AAAAD, LOOK!
I THINK HE'S LUCKY!
THAT'S STRANGE, IT LOOKS LIKE A BIRD- BUT THE TINIEST ONE I'VE EVER SEEN!

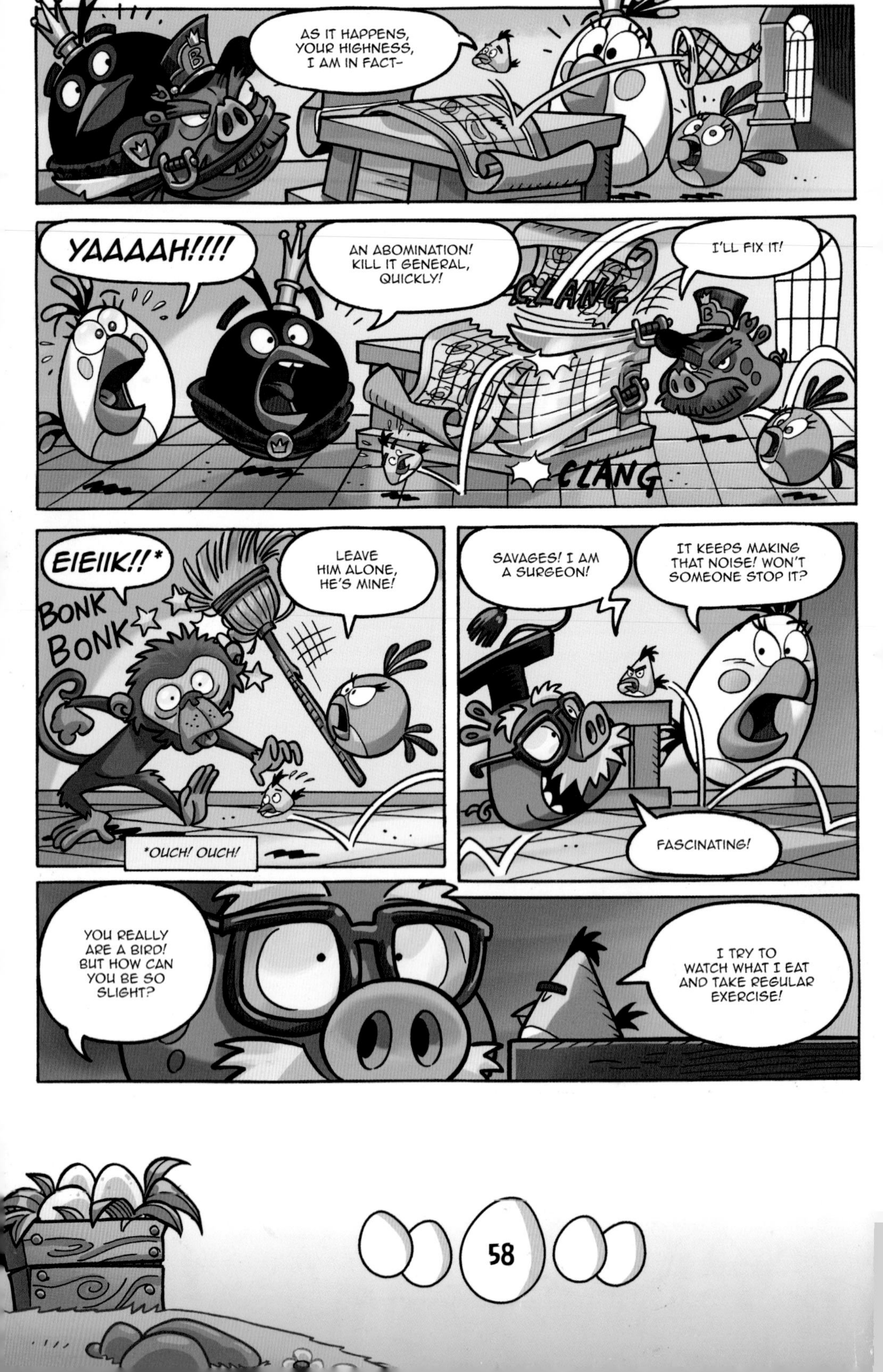
AS IT HAPPENS, YOUR HIGHNESS, I AM IN FACT-
YAAAAH!!!!
AN ABOMINATION! KILL IT GENERAL, QUICKLY!
CLANG
I'LL FIX IT!
CLANG
EIEIIK!! *
BONK BONK
LEAVE HIM ALONE, HE'S MINE!
*OUCH! OUCH!
SAVAGES! I AM A SURGEON!
IT KEEPS MAKING THAT NOISE! WON'T SOMEONE STOP IT?
FASCINATING!
YOU REALLY ARE A BIRD! BUT HOW CAN YOU BE SO SLIGHT?
I TRY TO WATCH WHAT I EAT AND TAKE REGULAR EXERCISE!

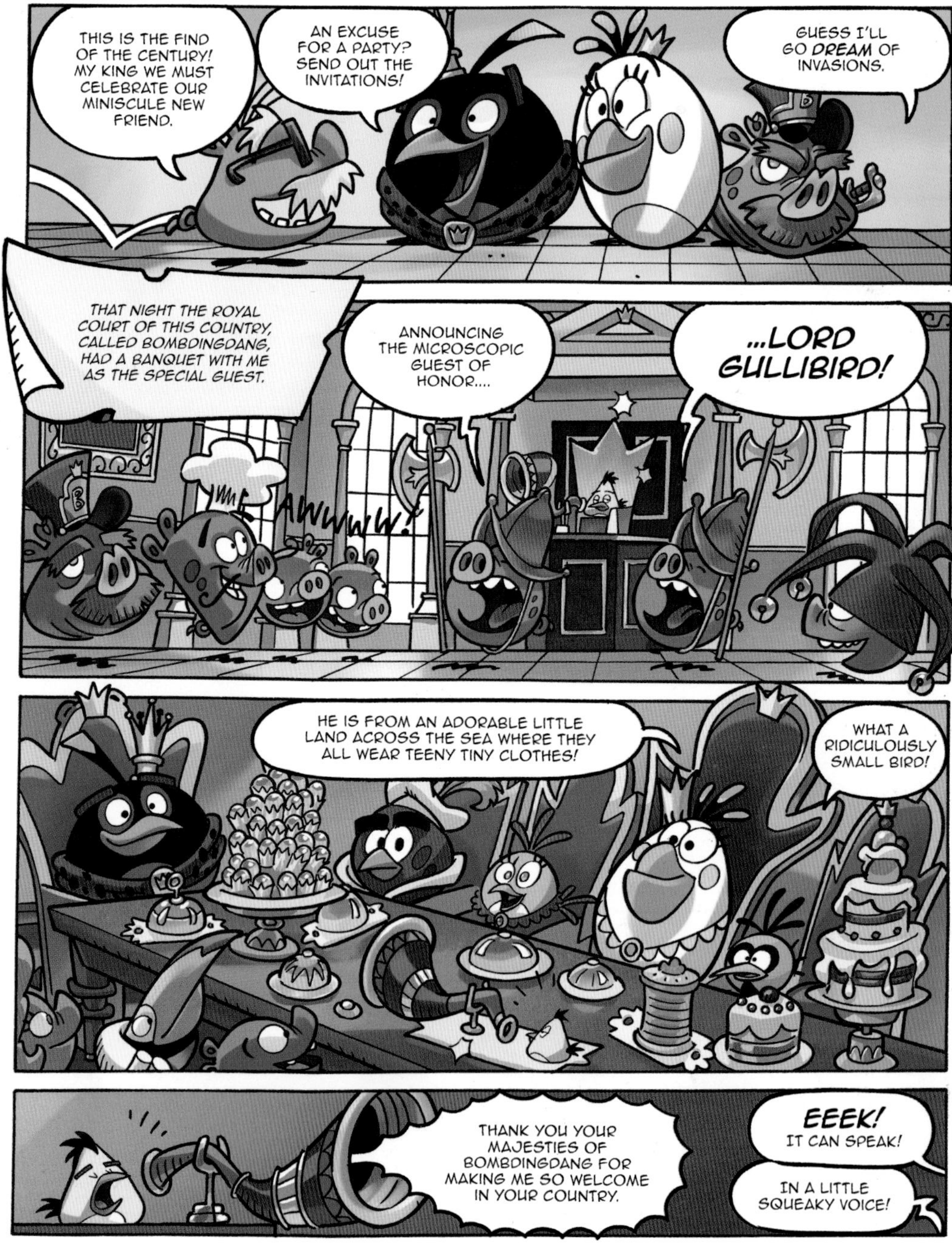
THIS IS THE FIND OF THE CENTURY! MY KING WE MUST CELEBRATE OUR MINISCULE NEW FRIEND.
AN EXCUSE FOR A PARTY? SEND OUT THE INVITATIONS!
GUESS I'LL GO DREAM OF INVASIONS.
THAT NIGHT THE ROYAL COURT OF THIS COUNTRY, CALLED BOMBDINGDANG, HAD A BANQUET WITH ME AS THE SPECIAL GUEST.
ANNOUNCING THE MICROSCOPIC GUEST OF HONOR....
...LORD GULLIBIRD!
AWWWW!
HE IS FROM AN ADORABLE LITTLE LAND ACROSS THE SEA WHERE THEY ALL WEAR TEENY TINY CLOTHES!
WHAT A RIDICULOUSLY SMALL BIRD!
THANK YOU YOUR MAJESTIES OF BOMBDINGDANG FOR MAKING ME SO WELCOME IN YOUR COUNTRY.
EEEK! IT CAN SPEAK!
IN A LITTLE SQUEAKY VOICE!

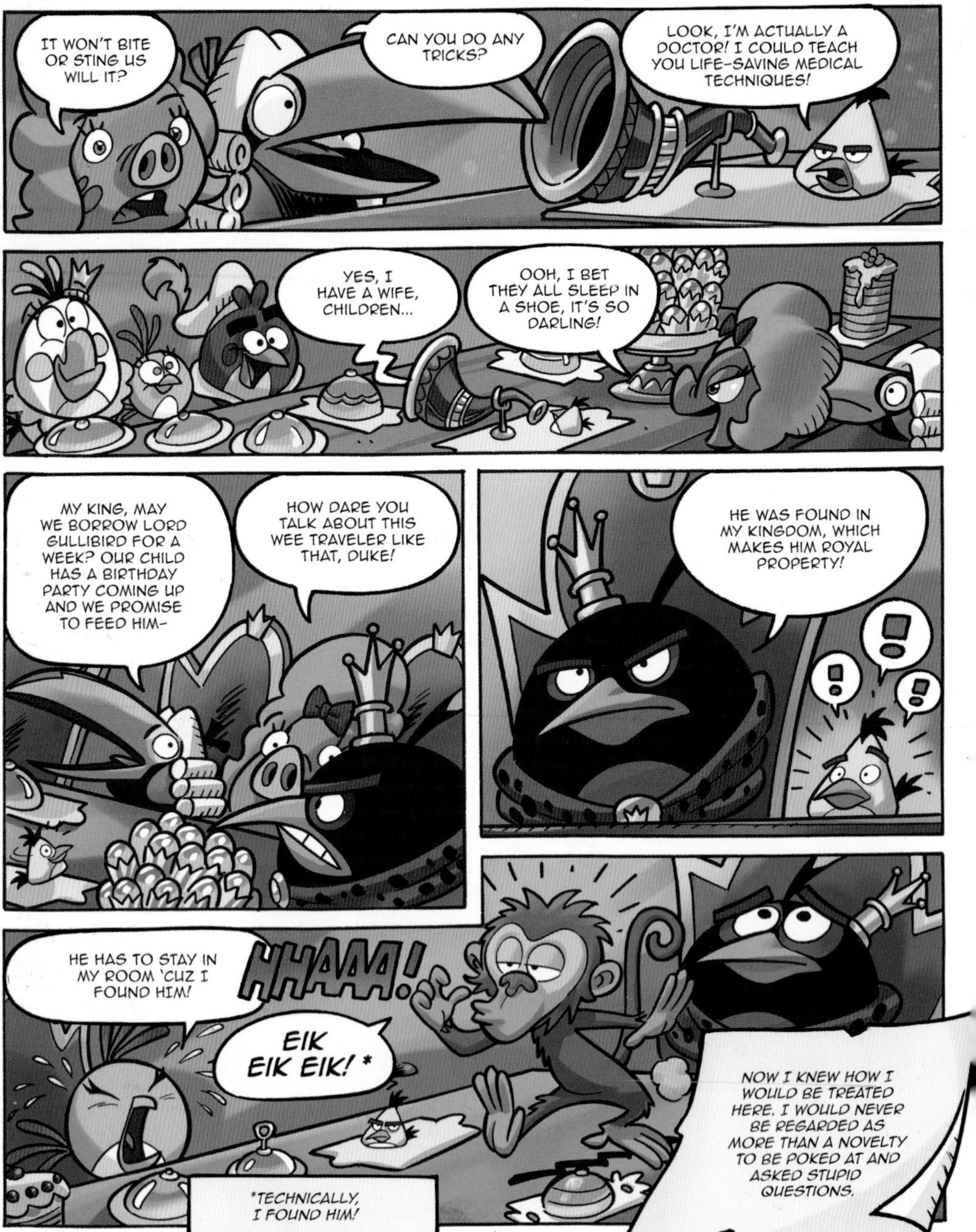
IT WON'T BITE OR STING US WILL IT?
CAN YOU DO ANY TRICKS?
LOOK, I'M ACTUALLY A DOCTOR! I COULD TEACH YOU LIFE-SAVING MEDICAL TECHNIQUES!
YES, I HAVE A WIFE, CHILDREN...
OOH, I BET THEY ALL SLEEP IN A SHOE, IT'S SO DARLING!
MY KING, MAY WE BORROW LORD GULLIBIRD FOR A WEEK? OUR CHILD HAS A BIRTHDAY PARTY COMING UP AND WE PROMISE TO FEED HIM-
HOW DARE YOU TALK ABOUT THIS WEE TRAVELER LIKE THAT, DUKE!
HE WAS FOUND IN MY KINGDOM, WHICH MAKES HIM ROYAL PROPERTY!
HE HAS TO STAY IN MY ROOM 'CUZ I FOUND HIM!
HHAAA!
EIK EIK EIK! *
*TECHNICALLY, I FOUND HIM!
NOW I KNEW HOW I WOULD BE TREATED HERE. I WOULD NEVER BE REGARDED AS MORE THAN A NOVELTY TO BE POKED AT AND ASKED STUPID QUESTIONS.

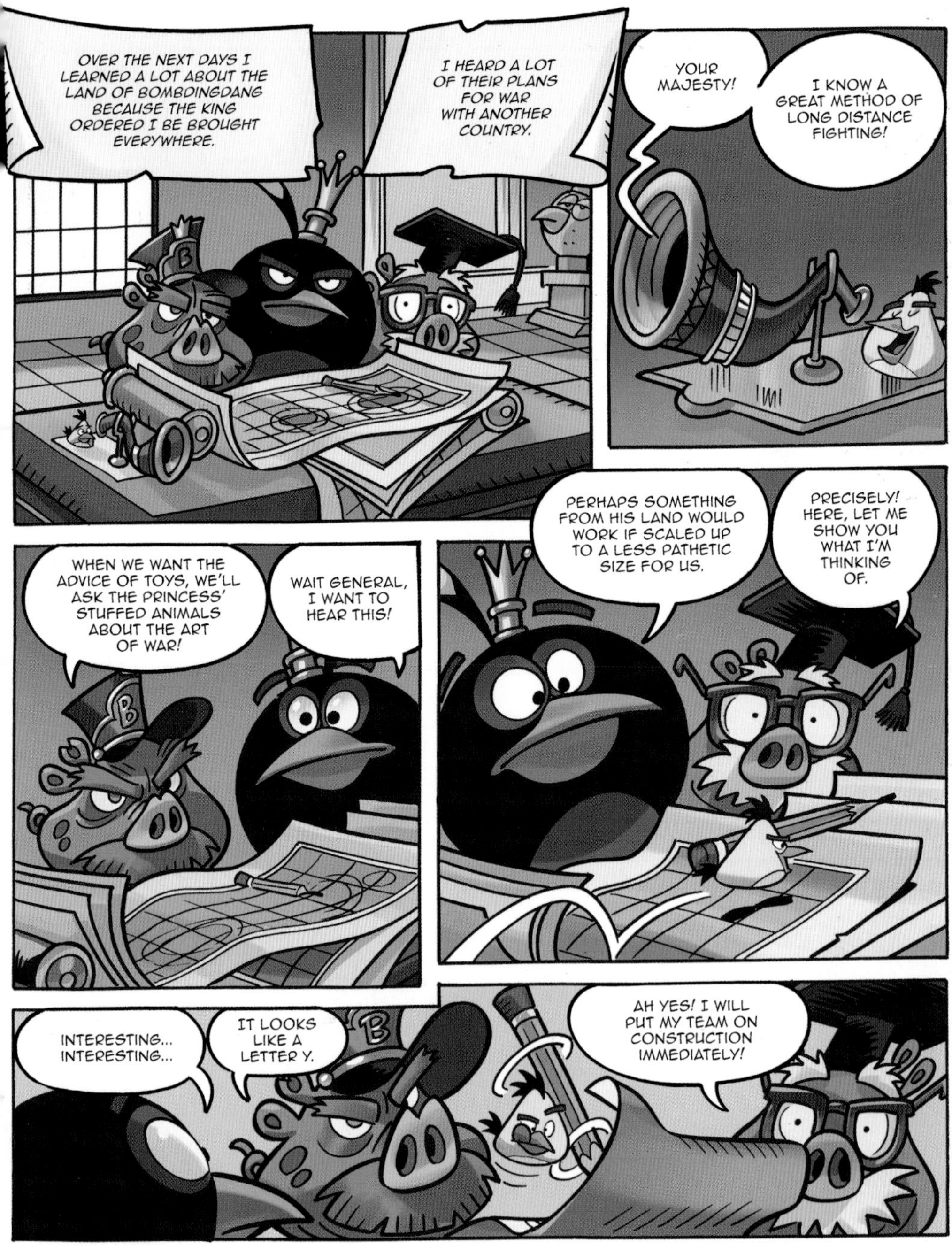
OVER THE NEXT DAYS I LEARNED A LOT ABOUT THE LAND OF BOMBDINGDANG BECAUSE THE KING ORDERED I BE BROUGHT EVERYWHERE.
I HEARD A LOT OF THEIR PLANS FOR WAR WITH ANOTHER COUNTRY.
YOUR MAJESTY!
I KNOW A GREAT METHOD OF LONG DISTANCE FIGHTING!
WHEN WE WANT THE ADVICE OF TOYS, WE'LL ASK THE PRINCESS' STUFFED ANIMALS ABOUT THE ART OF WAR!
WAIT GENERAL, I WANT TO HEAR THIS!
PERHAPS SOMETHING FROM HIS LAND WOULD WORK IF SCALED UP TO A LESS PATHETIC SIZE FOR US.
PRECISELY! HERE, LET ME SHOW YOU WHAT I'M THINKING OF.
INTERESTING... INTERESTING...
IT LOOKS LIKE A LETTER Y.
AH YES! I WILL PUT MY TEAM ON CONSTRUCTION IMMEDIATELY!

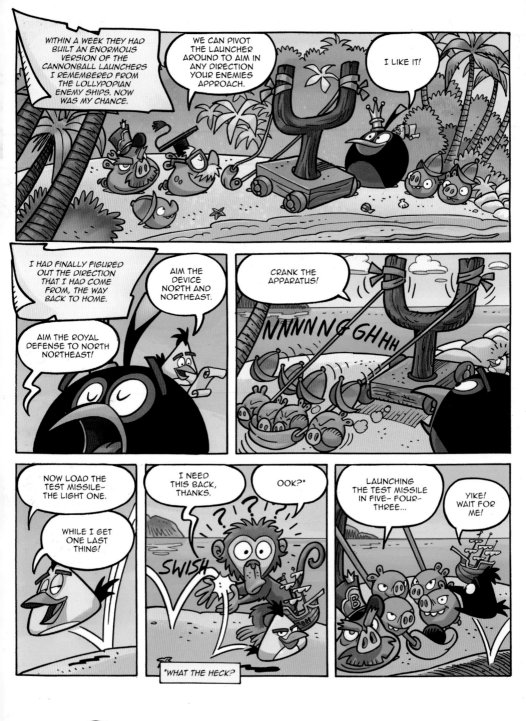

WITHIN A WEEK THEY HAD BUILT AN ENORMOUS VERSION OF THE CANNONBALL LAUNCHERS I REMEMBERED FROM THE LOLLYPOPIAN ENEMY SHIPS. NOW WAS MY CHANCE.

WE CAN PIVOT THE LAUNCHER AROUND TO AIM IN ANY DIRECTION YOUR ENEMIES APPROACH.

I LIKE IT!

I HAD FINALLY FIGURED OUT THE DIRECTION THAT I HAD COME FROM, THE WAY BACK TO HOME.

AIM THE DEVICE NORTH AND NORTHEAST.

AIM THE ROYAL DEFENSE TO NORTH NORTHEAST!

CRANK THE APPARATUS!

NNNNNGGHHH

NOW LOAD THE TEST MISSILE- THE LIGHT ONE.

WHILE I GET ONE LAST THING!

I NEED THIS BACK, THANKS.

OOK?*

SWISH

*WHAT THE HECK?

LAUNCHING THE TEST MISSILE IN FIVE- FOUR- THREE...

YIKE! WAIT FOR ME!

62

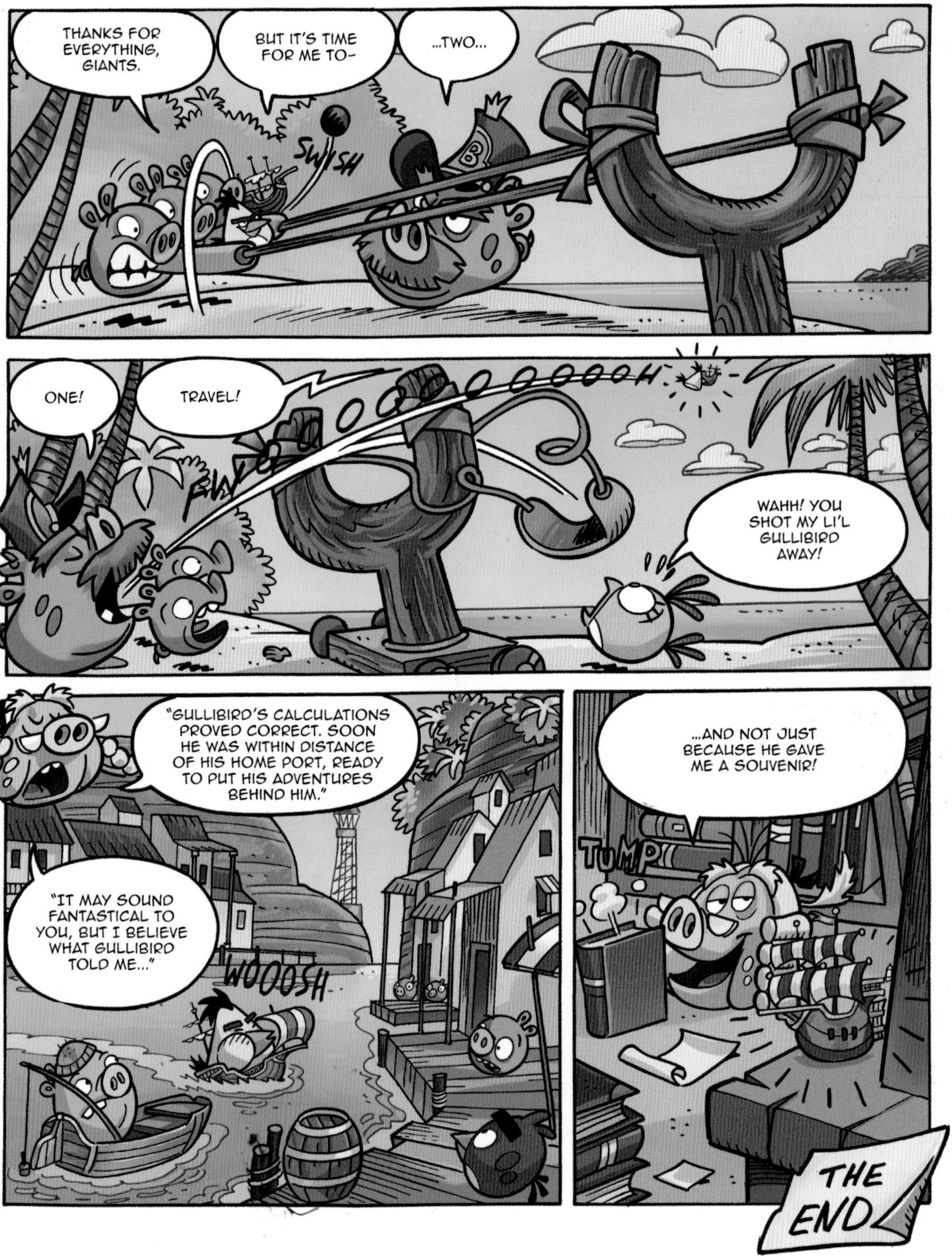
THANKS FOR EVERYTHING, GIANTS.
BUT IT'S TIME FOR ME TO-
...TWO...
SWISH
ONE!
TRAVEL!
FWOOOOOOOOOOOOOOH
WAHH! YOU SHOT MY LI'L GULLIBIRD AWAY!
"GULLIBIRD'S CALCULATIONS PROVED CORRECT. SOON HE WAS WITHIN DISTANCE OF HIS HOME PORT, READY TO PUT HIS ADVENTURES BEHIND HIM."
"IT MAY SOUND FANTASTICAL TO YOU, BUT I BELIEVE WHAT GULLIBIRD TOLD ME..."
WOOOSH
...AND NOT JUST BECAUSE HE GAVE ME A SOUVENIR!
TUMP
THE END

BAD PIGGIES
CHEF IN THE SOUP
HERE COMES YOUR MORNING GRASS, YOUR BOARNESS.
SIGH. JUST LEAVE IT ON THE TABLE.
AB 2014-013
BON APPETITE, YOUR PIGNESS!
YEAH, RIGHT.
AUUUGH!
WHAT'S WRONG, YOUR BACONESS?
MY TOOTH! CALL A DOCTOR!
I'D SAY THERE'S SOMETHING WRONG WITH YOUR TOOTH, YOUR PIGGINESS.
WHAT SHOULD I DO?
I GUESS THAT YOU SHOULD EAT ONLY SOUP AND HOPE THAT THE PAIN GOES AWAY.
SOUP?
SOUP? THAT SOUNDS YUMMY!

WRITTEN BY: JANNE TORISEVA • ART BY: JEAN-MICHEL BOESCH • COLORS BY: DIGIKORE • LETTERS BY: PISARA OY

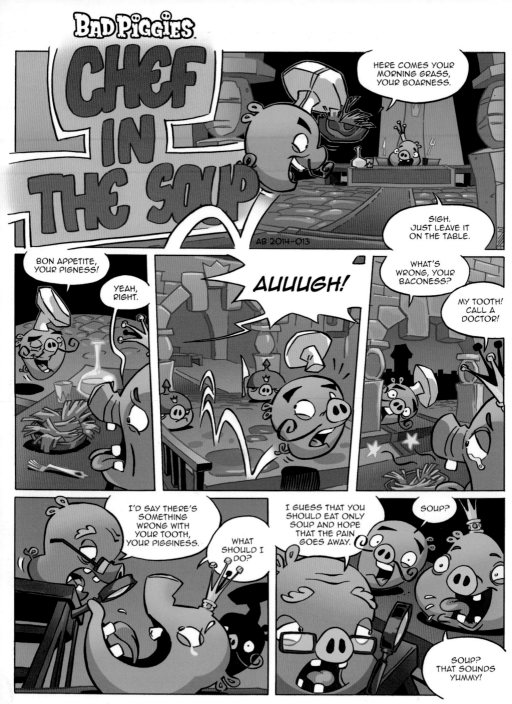

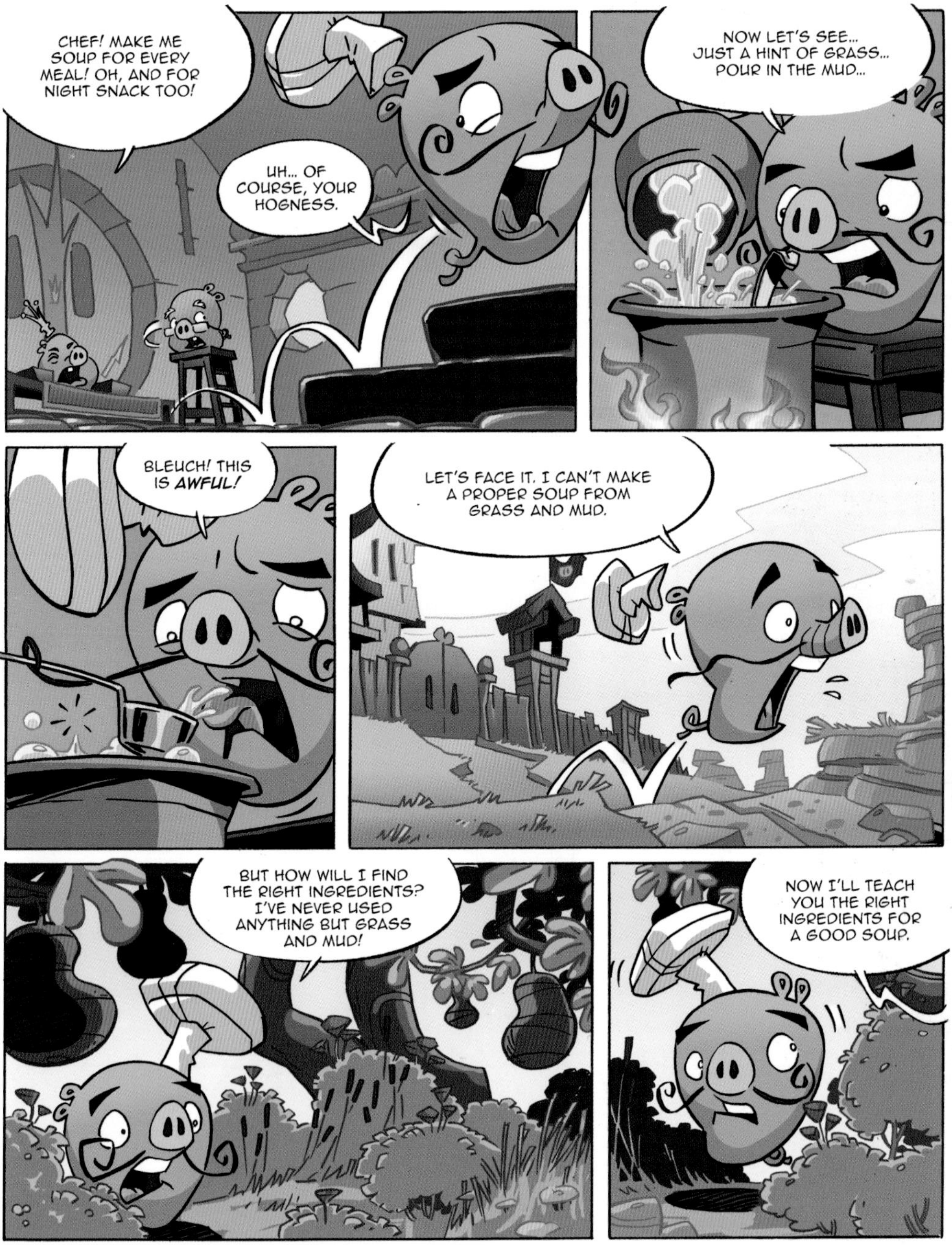
CHEF! MAKE ME SOUP FOR EVERY MEAL! OH, AND FOR NIGHT SNACK TOO!
UH... OF COURSE, YOUR HOGNESS.
NOW LET'S SEE... JUST A HINT OF GRASS... POUR IN THE MUD...
BLEUCH! THIS IS *AWFUL!*
LET'S FACE IT. I CAN'T MAKE A PROPER SOUP FROM GRASS AND MUD.
BUT HOW WILL I FIND THE RIGHT INGREDIENTS? I'VE NEVER USED ANYTHING BUT GRASS AND MUD!
NOW I'LL TEACH YOU THE RIGHT INGREDIENTS FOR A GOOD SOUP.

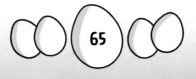

ADD A FEW OF THESE AND A COUPLE OF THOSE...
...BUT REMEMBER THAT THE MOST IMPORTANT INGREDIENT IS THIS SMALL, PURPLE LEAF.
SNIFF! WHAT A DELICIOUS SMELL!
A FEW OF THESE AND A COUPLE OF THOSE...
...AND THE KING SHOULD HAVE ONE MAGNIFICENT SOUP!

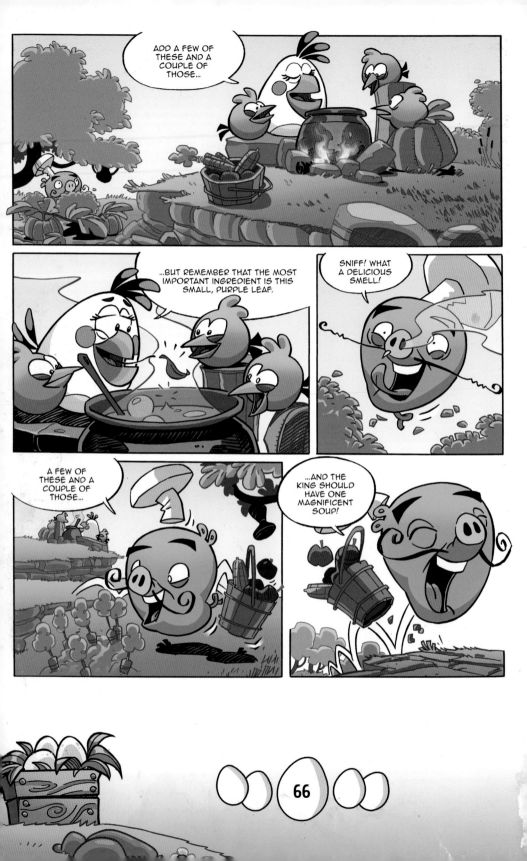

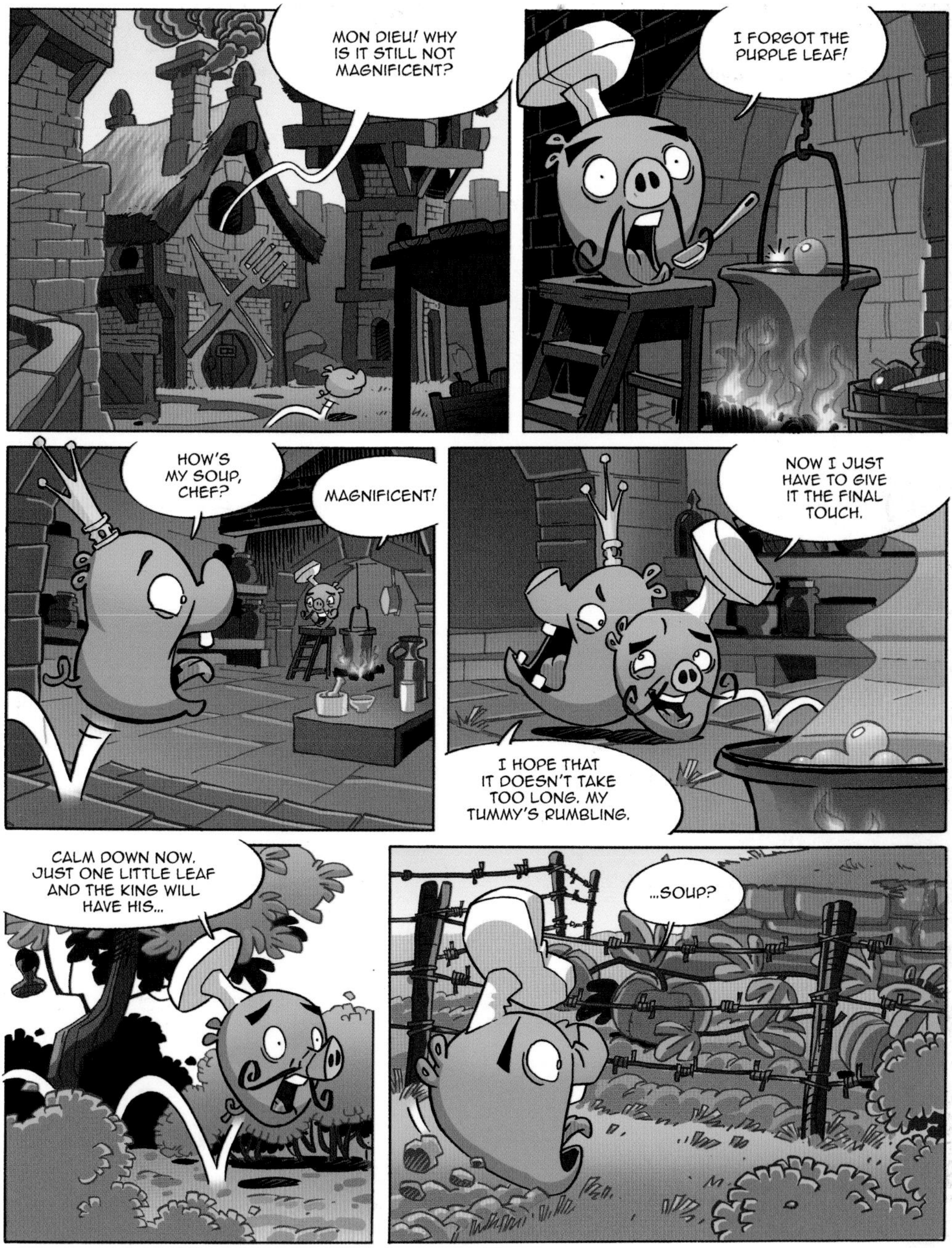
MON DIEU! WHY IS IT STILL NOT MAGNIFICENT?
I FORGOT THE PURPLE LEAF!
HOW'S MY SOUP, CHEF?
MAGNIFICENT!
NOW I JUST HAVE TO GIVE IT THE FINAL TOUCH.
I HOPE THAT IT DOESN'T TAKE TOO LONG. MY TUMMY'S RUMBLING.
CALM DOWN NOW. JUST ONE LITTLE LEAF AND THE KING WILL HAVE HIS...
...SOUP?

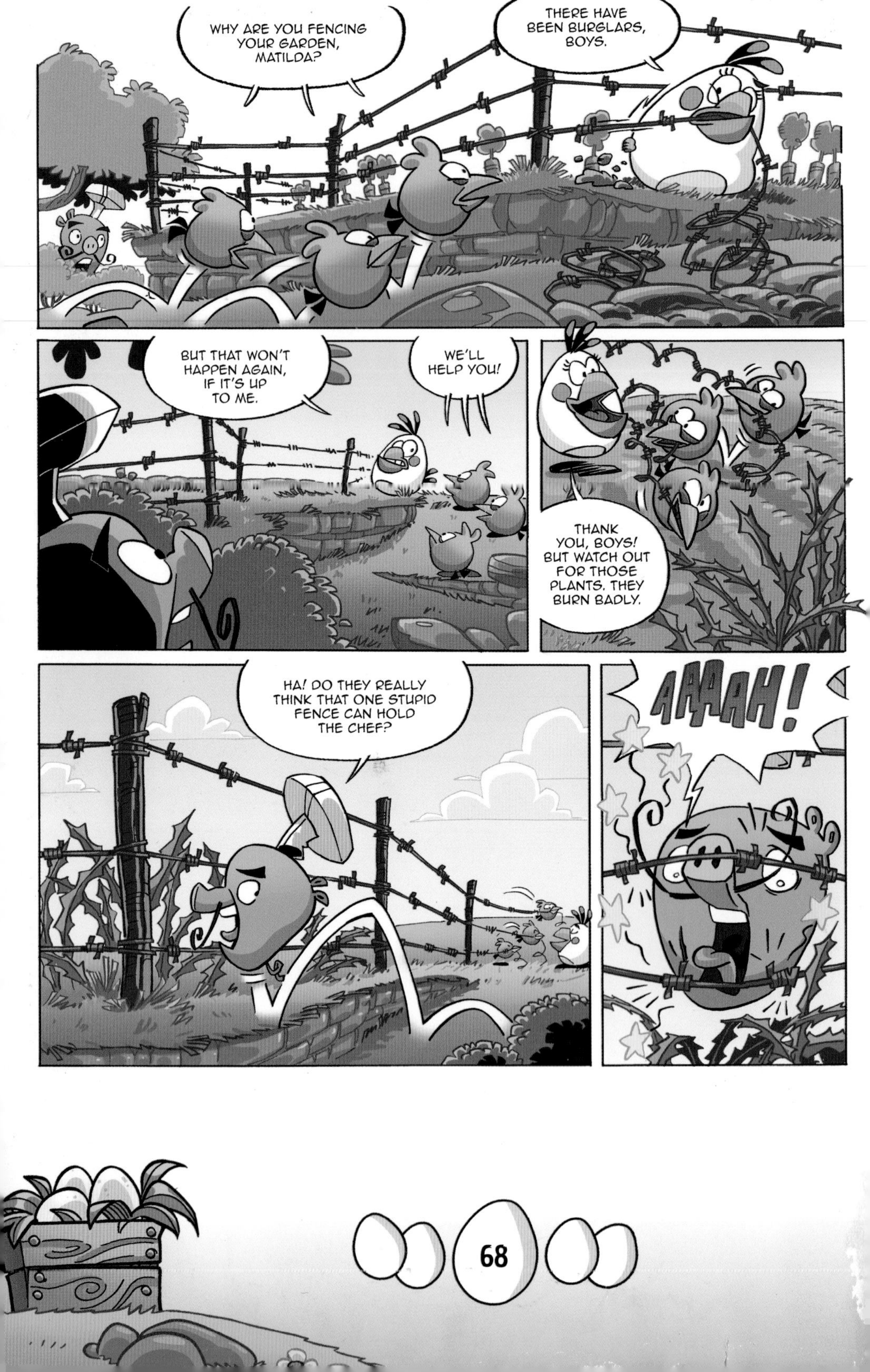
WHY ARE YOU FENCING YOUR GARDEN, MATILDA?
THERE HAVE BEEN BURGLARS, BOYS.
BUT THAT WON'T HAPPEN AGAIN, IF IT'S UP TO ME.
WE'LL HELP YOU!
THANK YOU, BOYS! BUT WATCH OUT FOR THOSE PLANTS. THEY BURN BADLY.
HA! DO THEY REALLY THINK THAT ONE STUPID FENCE CAN HOLD THE CHEF?
AAAAH!

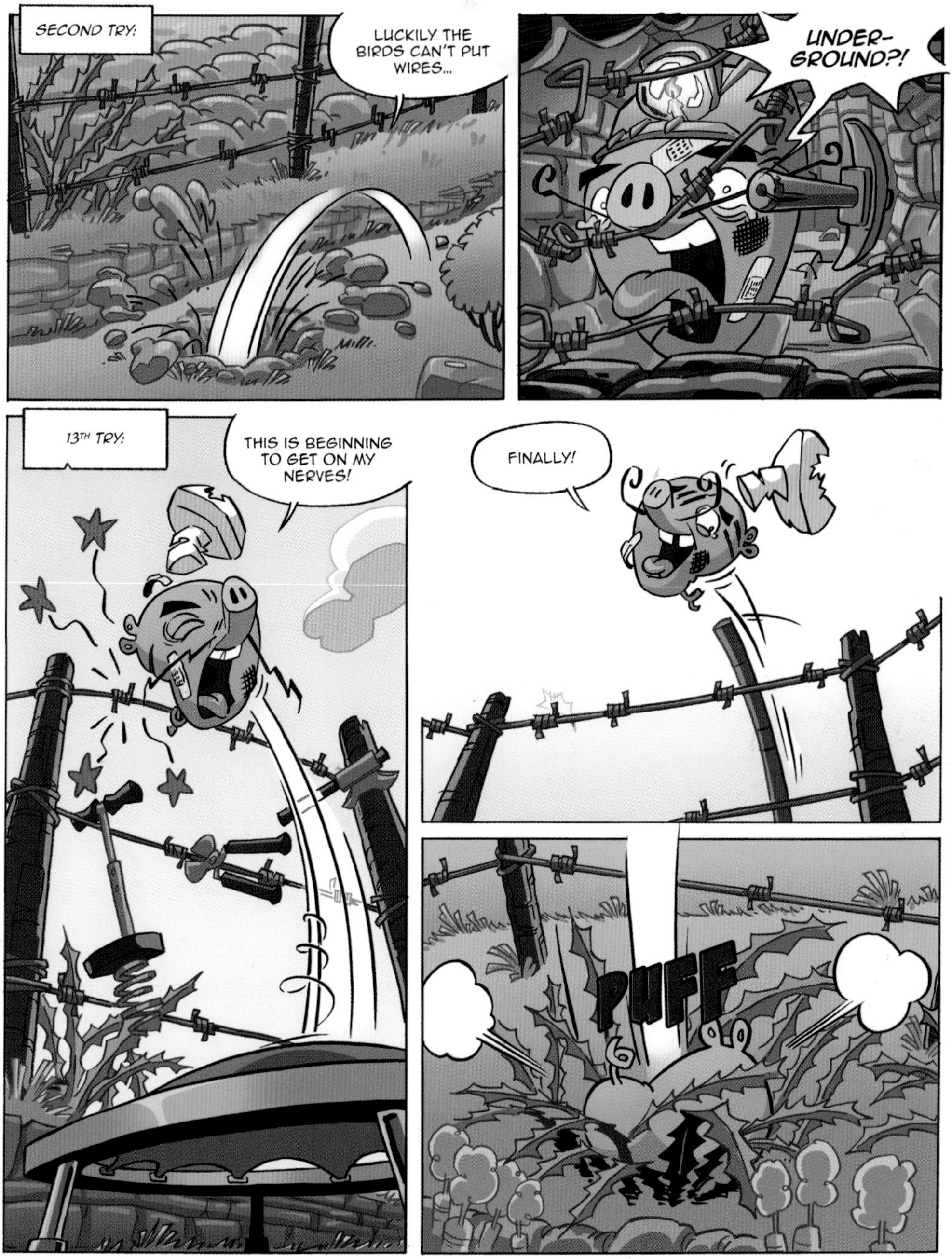
SECOND TRY:
LUCKILY THE BIRDS CAN'T PUT WIRES...
UNDER-GROUND?!
13TH TRY:
THIS IS BEGINNING TO GET ON MY NERVES!
FINALLY!
PUFF

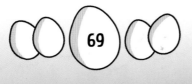

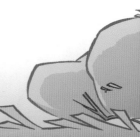

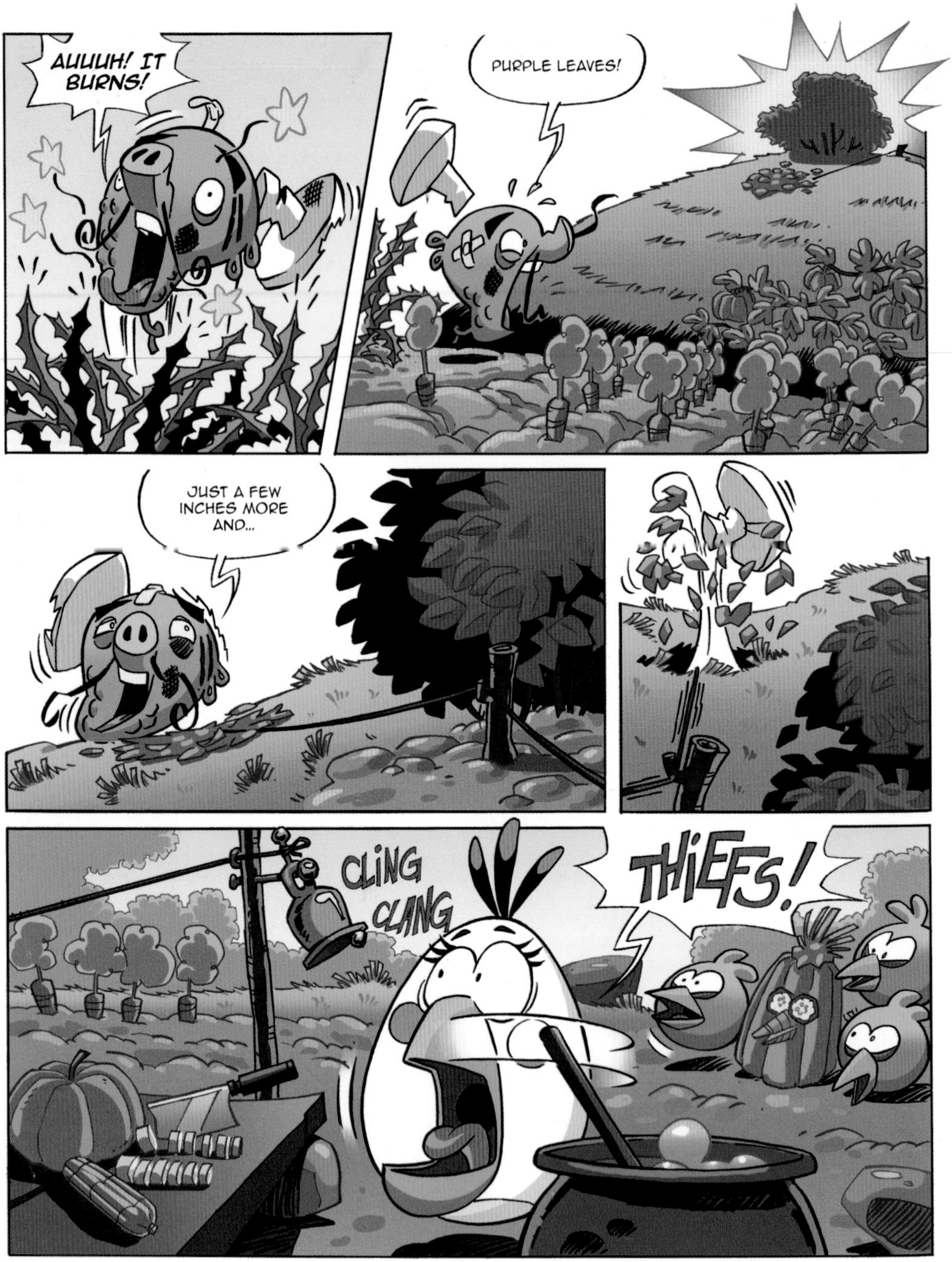
AUUUH! IT BURNS!
PURPLE LEAVES!
JUST A FEW INCHES MORE AND...
CLING
CLANG
THIEFS!

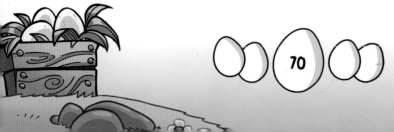

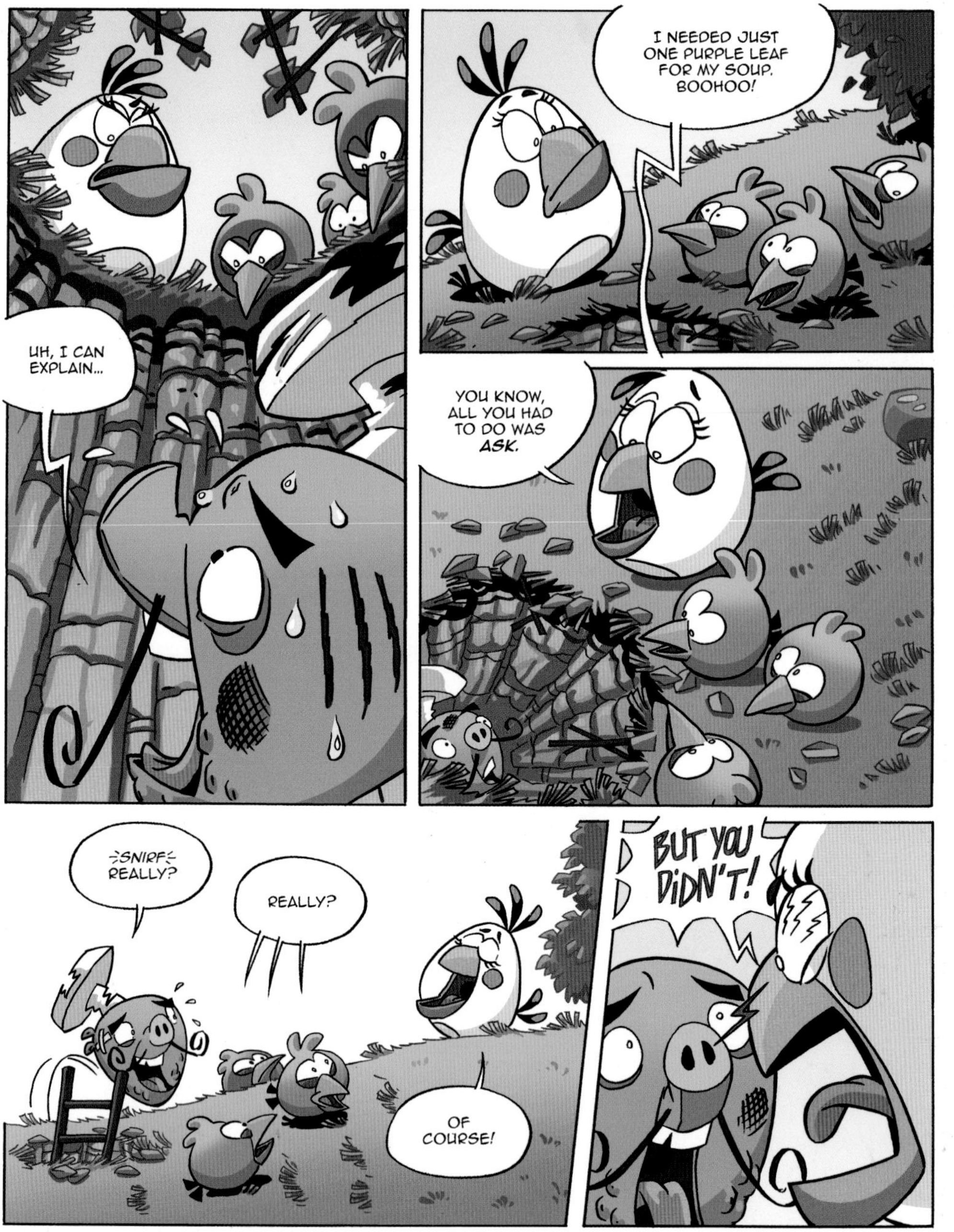
UH, I CAN EXPLAIN...
I NEEDED JUST ONE PURPLE LEAF FOR MY SOUP. BOOHOO!
YOU KNOW, ALL YOU HAD TO DO WAS ASK.
SNIRF REALLY?
REALLY?
OF COURSE!
BUT YOU DIDN'T!

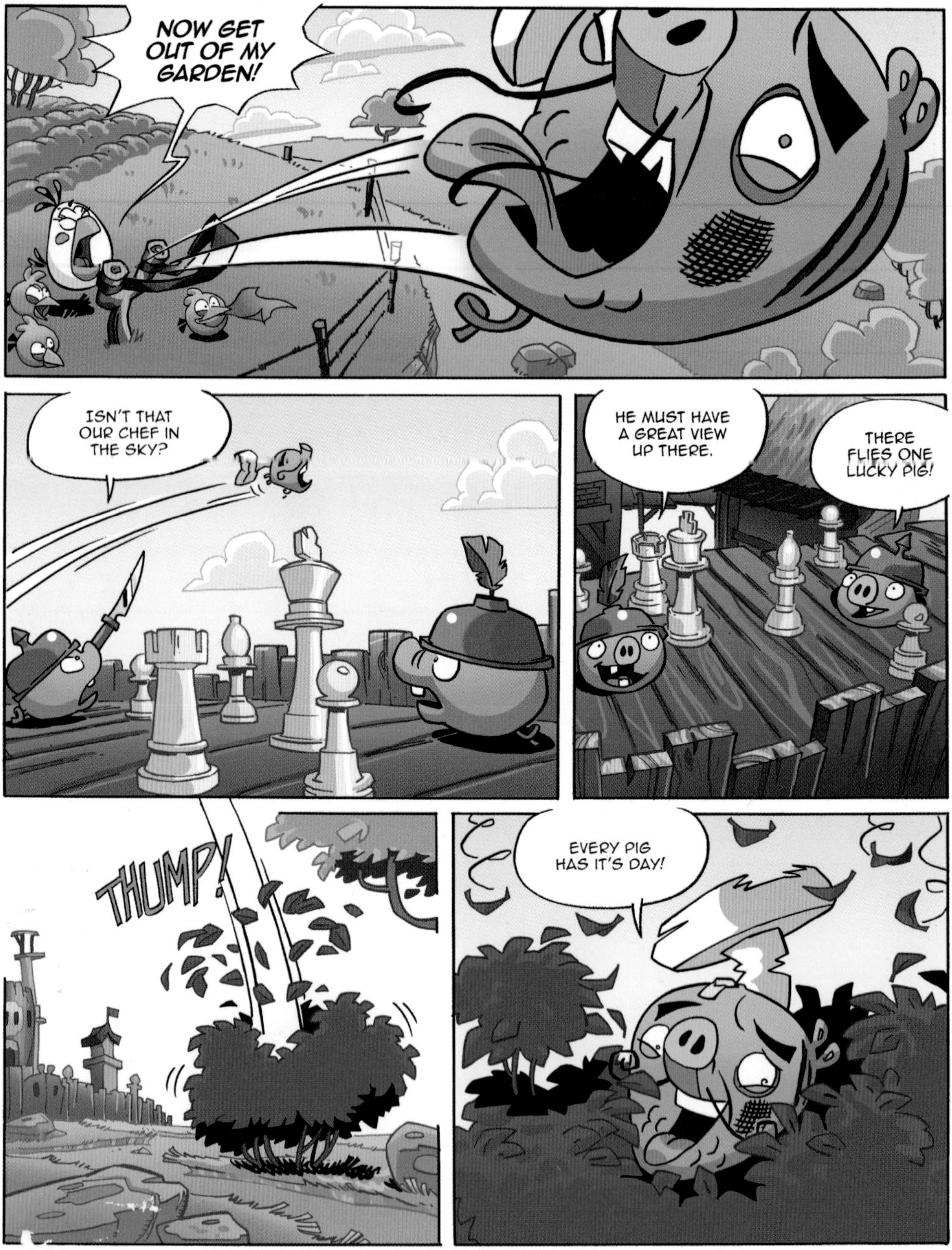
NOW GET OUT OF MY GARDEN!
ISN'T THAT OUR CHEF IN THE SKY?
HE MUST HAVE A GREAT VIEW UP THERE.
THERE FLIES ONE LUCKY PIG!
THUMP!
EVERY PIG HAS IT'S DAY!

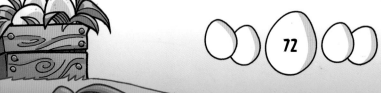

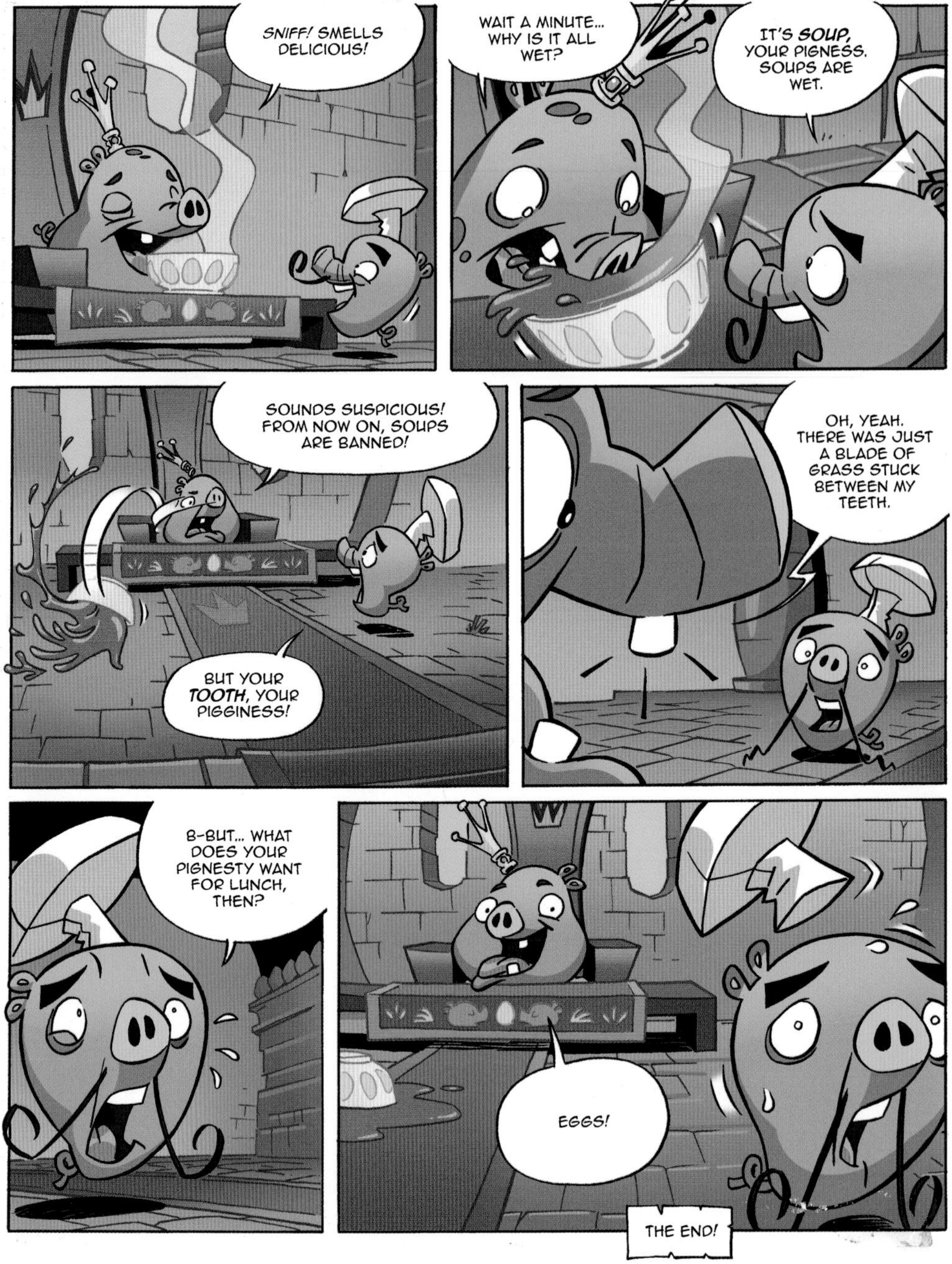
SNIFF! SMELLS DELICIOUS!
WAIT A MINUTE... WHY IS IT ALL WET?
IT'S SOUP, YOUR PIGNESS. SOUPS ARE WET.
SOUNDS SUSPICIOUS! FROM NOW ON, SOUPS ARE BANNED!
BUT YOUR TOOTH, YOUR PIGGINESS!
OH, YEAH. THERE WAS JUST A BLADE OF GRASS STUCK BETWEEN MY TEETH.
B-BUT... WHAT DOES YOUR PIGNESTY WANT FOR LUNCH, THEN?
EGGS!
THE END!

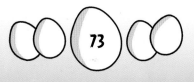

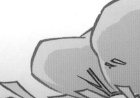

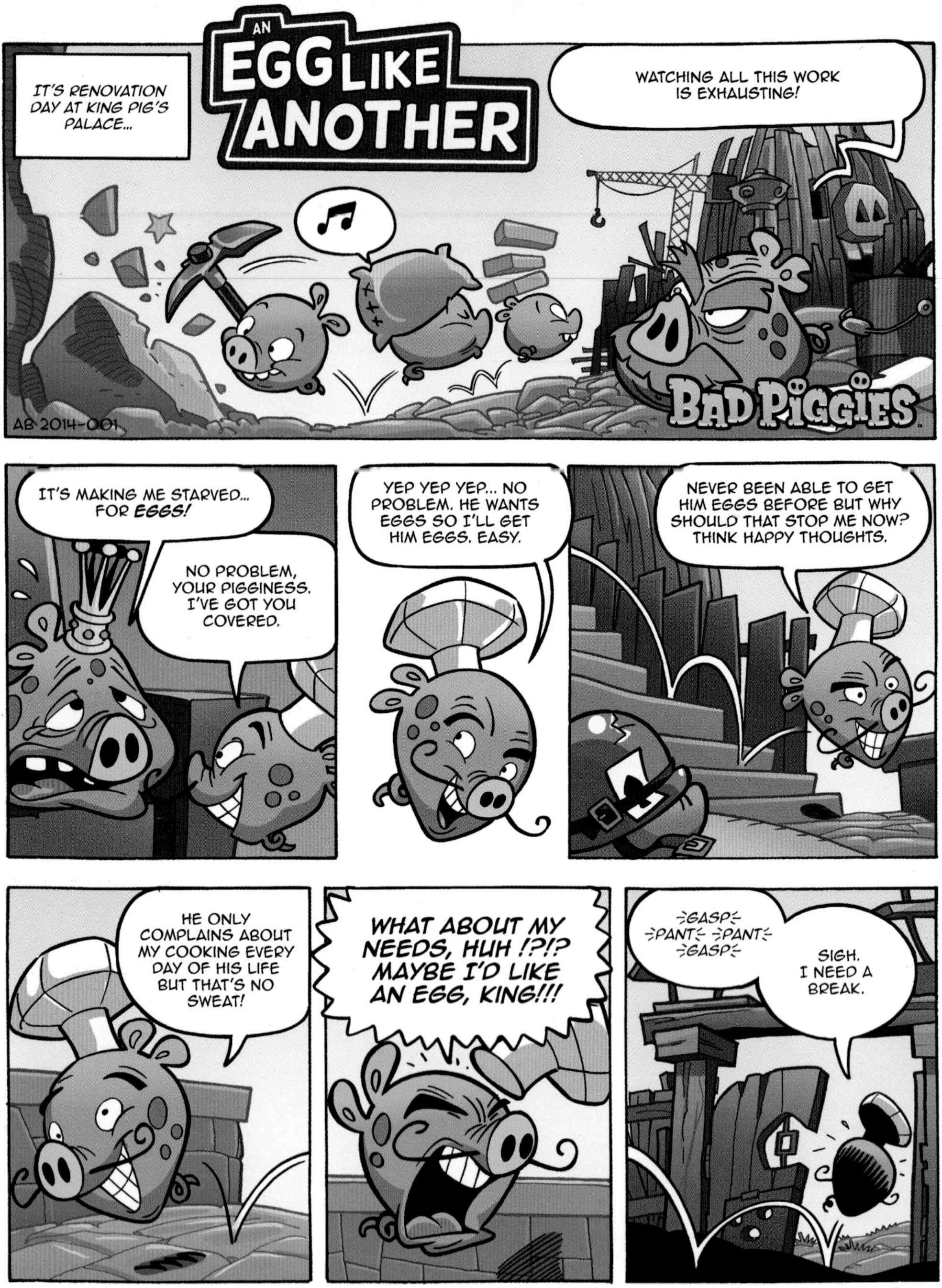
AN EGG LIKE ANOTHER
IT'S RENOVATION DAY AT KING PIG'S PALACE...
WATCHING ALL THIS WORK IS EXHAUSTING!
AB 2014-001
BAD PIGGIES
IT'S MAKING ME STARVED... FOR EGGS!
NO PROBLEM, YOUR PIGGINESS. I'VE GOT YOU COVERED.
YEP YEP YEP... NO PROBLEM. HE WANTS EGGS SO I'LL GET HIM EGGS. EASY.
NEVER BEEN ABLE TO GET HIM EGGS BEFORE BUT WHY SHOULD THAT STOP ME NOW? THINK HAPPY THOUGHTS.
HE ONLY COMPLAINS ABOUT MY COOKING EVERY DAY OF HIS LIFE BUT THAT'S NO SWEAT!
WHAT ABOUT MY NEEDS, HUH !?!? MAYBE I'D LIKE AN EGG, KING!!!
GASP PANT PANT GASP
SIGH. I NEED A BREAK.

WRITTEN BY: FRANÇOIS CORTEGGIANI • ART BY: GIORGIO CAVAZZANO AND A. ZEMOLIN • COLORS BY: DIGIKORE • LETTERS BY: PISARA OY

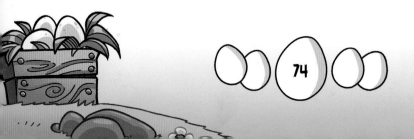

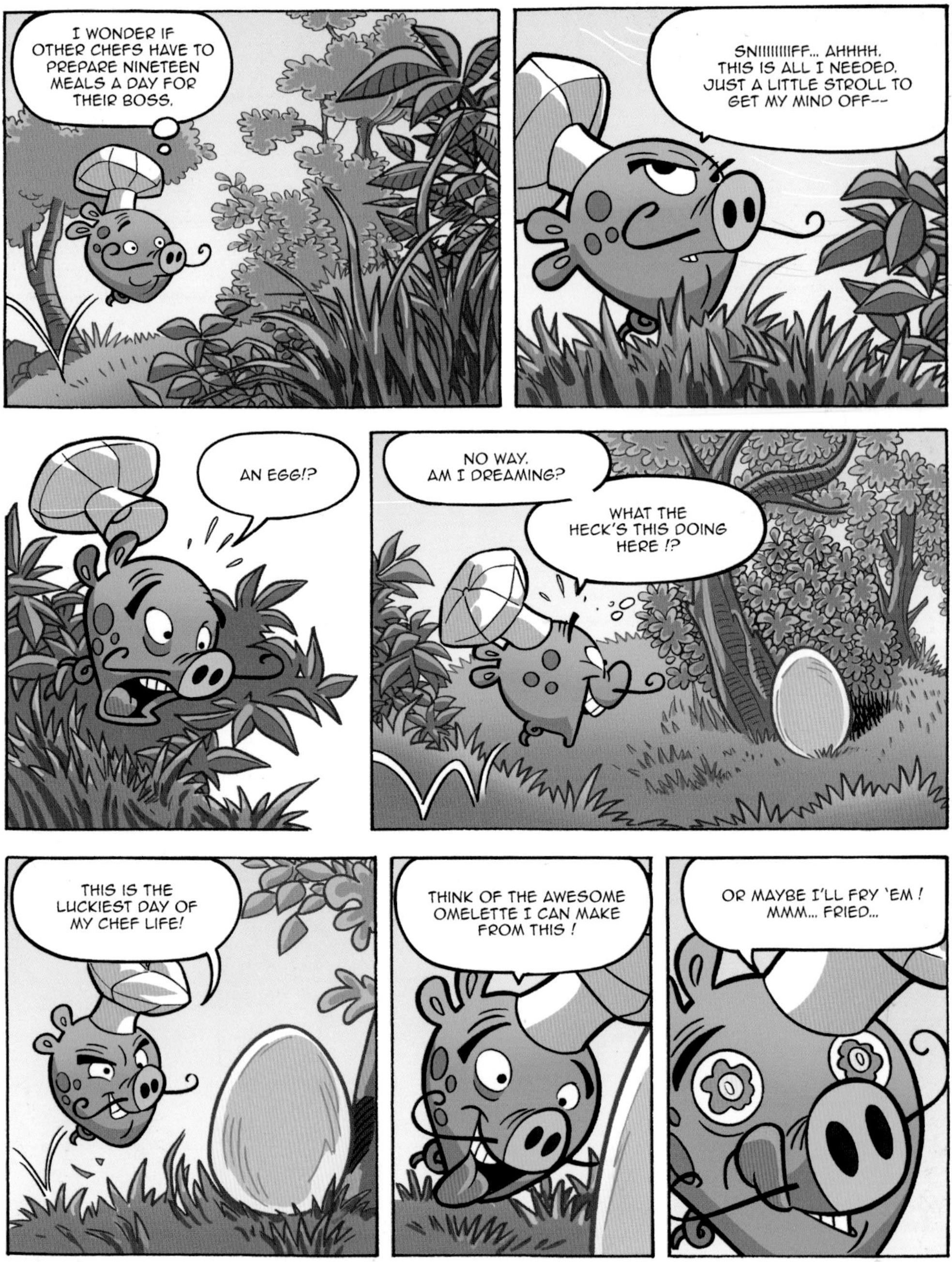
I WONDER IF OTHER CHEFS HAVE TO PREPARE NINETEEN MEALS A DAY FOR THEIR BOSS.
SNIIIIIIIFF... AHHHH. THIS IS ALL I NEEDED. JUST A LITTLE STROLL TO GET MY MIND OFF--
AN EGG!?
NO WAY. AM I DREAMING?
WHAT THE HECK'S THIS DOING HERE !?
THIS IS THE LUCKIEST DAY OF MY CHEF LIFE!
THINK OF THE AWESOME OMELETTE I CAN MAKE FROM THIS !
OR MAYBE I'LL FRY 'EM ! MMM... FRIED...

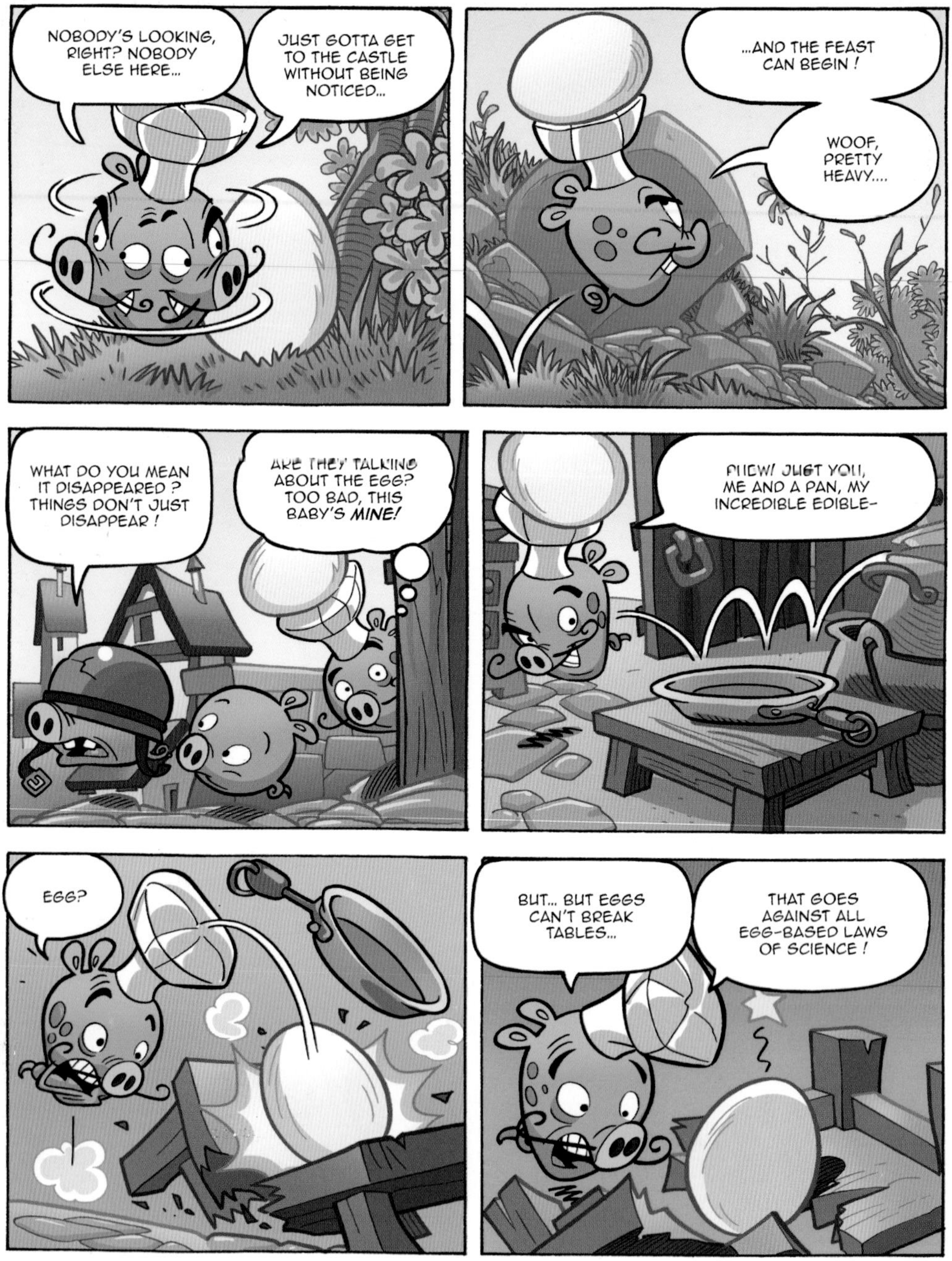
NOBODY'S LOOKING, RIGHT? NOBODY ELSE HERE...
JUST GOTTA GET TO THE CASTLE WITHOUT BEING NOTICED...
...AND THE FEAST CAN BEGIN !
WOOF, PRETTY HEAVY....
WHAT DO YOU MEAN IT DISAPPEARED ? THINGS DON'T JUST DISAPPEAR !
ARE THEY TALKING ABOUT THE EGG? TOO BAD, THIS BABY'S MINE!
PHEW! JUST YOU, ME AND A PAN, MY INCREDIBLE EDIBLE-
EGG?
BUT... BUT EGGS CAN'T BREAK TABLES...
THAT GOES AGAINST ALL EGG-BASED LAWS OF SCIENCE !

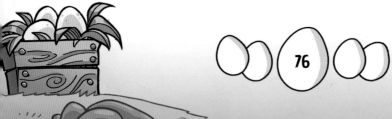

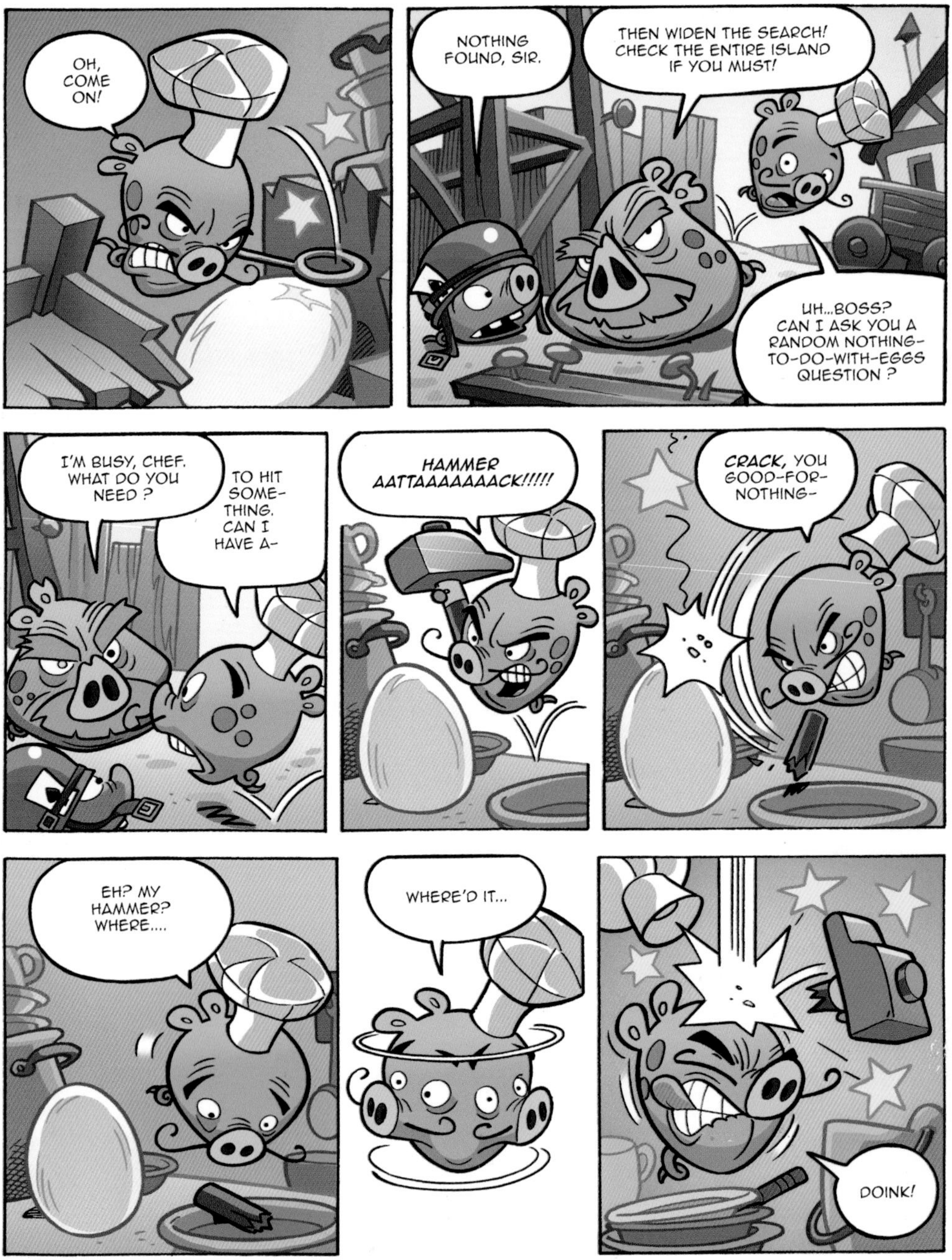
OH, COME ON!
NOTHING FOUND, SIR.
THEN WIDEN THE SEARCH! CHECK THE ENTIRE ISLAND IF YOU MUST!
UH...BOSS? CAN I ASK YOU A RANDOM NOTHING-TO-DO-WITH-EGGS QUESTION ?
I'M BUSY, CHEF. WHAT DO YOU NEED ?
TO HIT SOME-THING. CAN I HAVE A-
HAMMER AATTAAAAAAACK!!!!!
CRACK, YOU GOOD-FOR-NOTHING-
EH? MY HAMMER? WHERE....
WHERE'D IT...
DOINK!

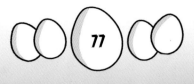

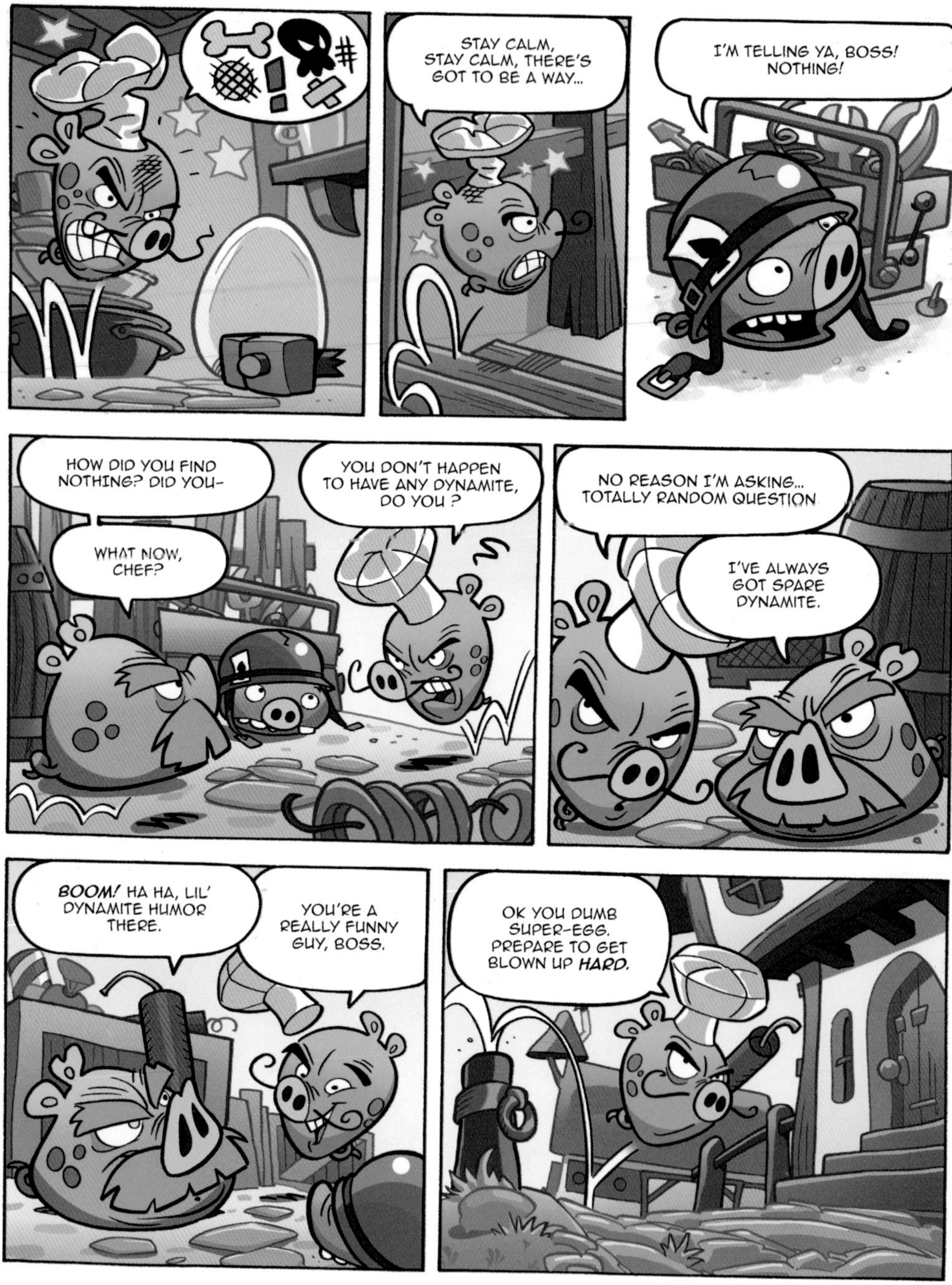
STAY CALM, STAY CALM, THERE'S GOT TO BE A WAY...
I'M TELLING YA, BOSS! NOTHING!
HOW DID YOU FIND NOTHING? DID YOU-
WHAT NOW, CHEF?
YOU DON'T HAPPEN TO HAVE ANY DYNAMITE, DO YOU ?
NO REASON I'M ASKING... TOTALLY RANDOM QUESTION
I'VE ALWAYS GOT SPARE DYNAMITE.
BOOM! HA HA, LIL' DYNAMITE HUMOR THERE.
YOU'RE A REALLY FUNNY GUY, BOSS.
OK YOU DUMB SUPER-EGG. PREPARE TO GET BLOWN UP HARD.

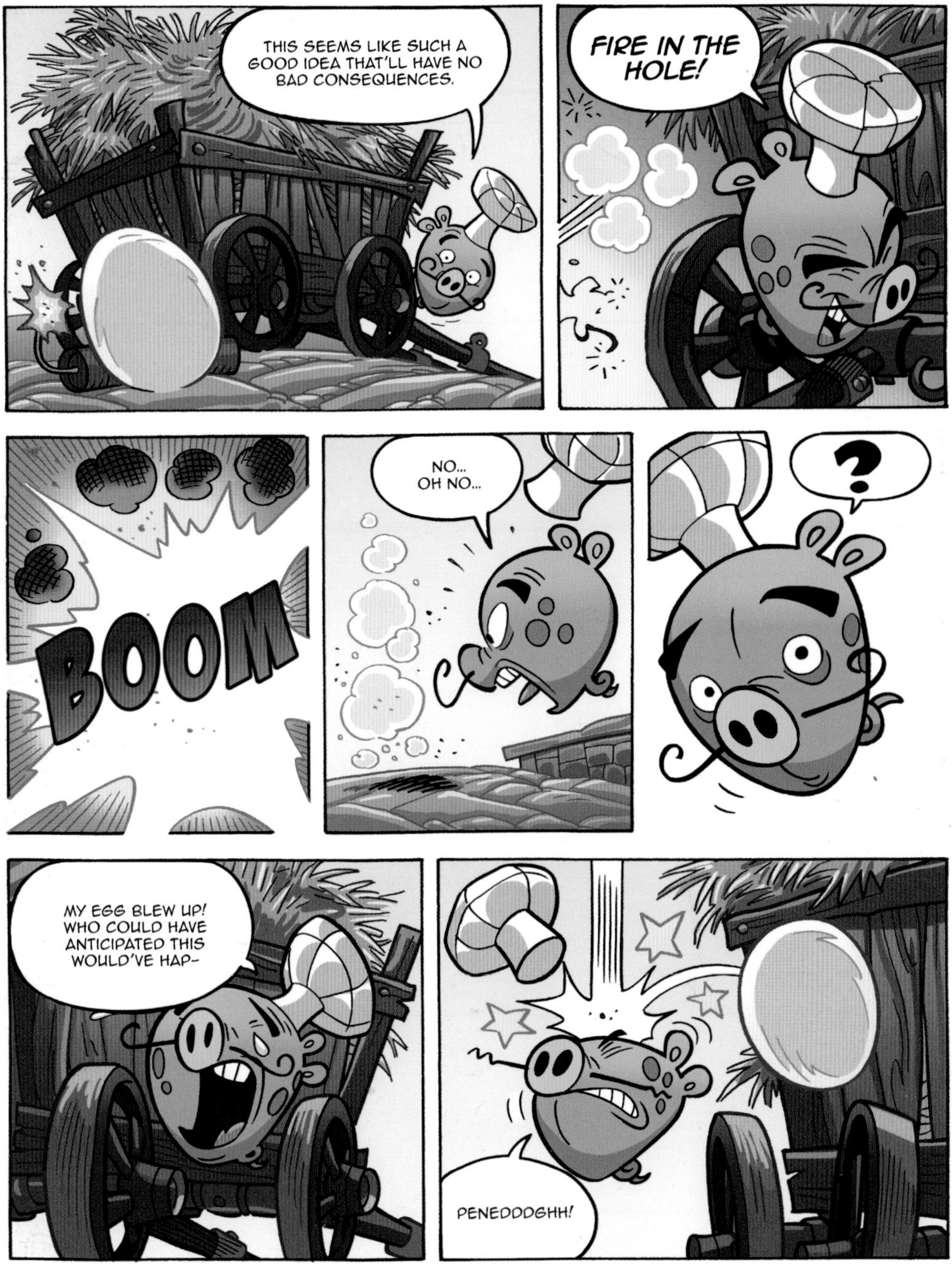
THIS SEEMS LIKE SUCH A GOOD IDEA THAT'LL HAVE NO BAD CONSEQUENCES.
FIRE IN THE HOLE!
BOOM
NO... OH NO...
?
MY EGG BLEW UP! WHO COULD HAVE ANTICIPATED THIS WOULD'VE HAP-
PENEDDDGHH!

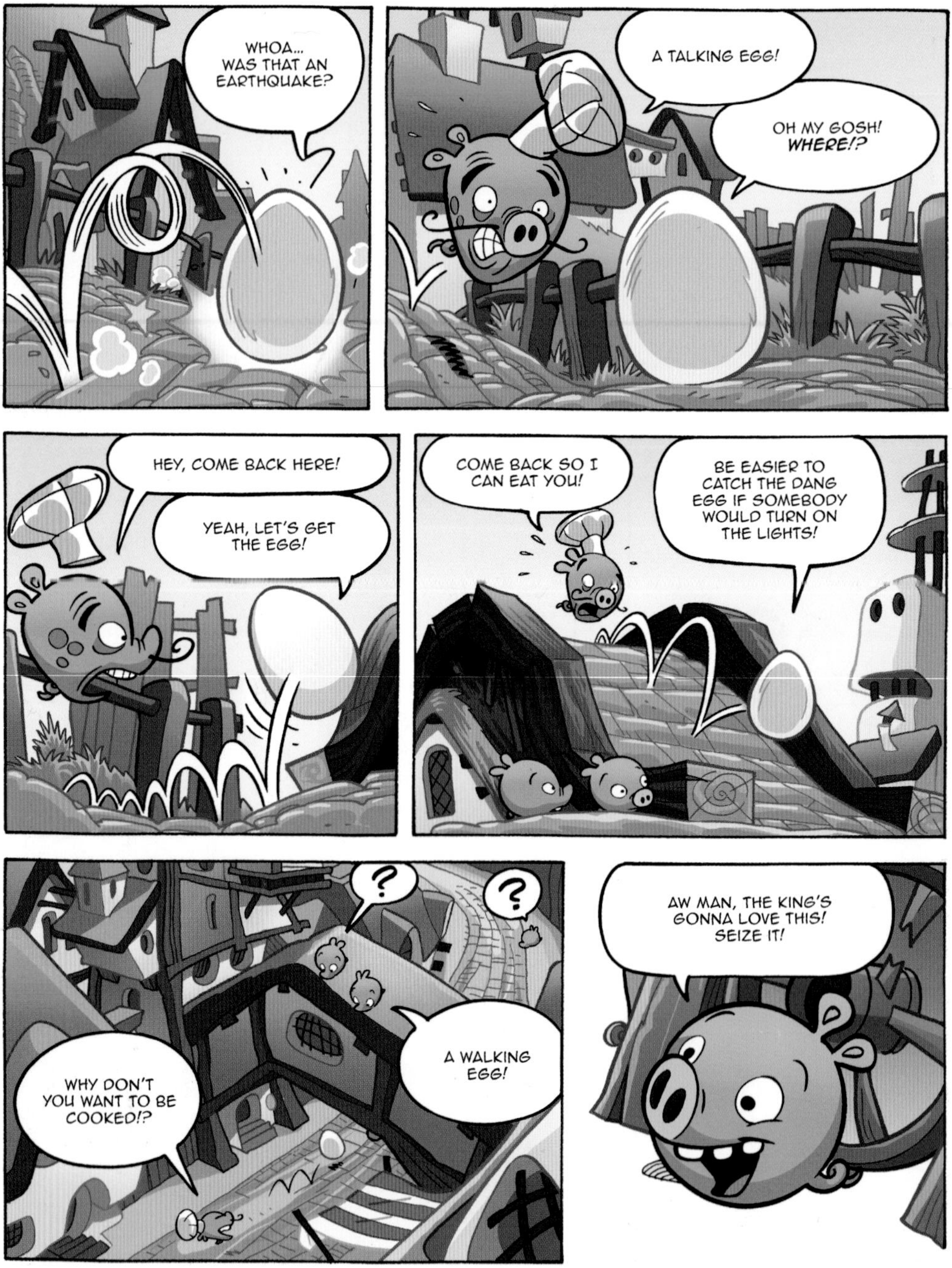
WHOA... WAS THAT AN EARTHQUAKE?
A TALKING EGG!
OH MY GOSH! *WHERE!?*
HEY, COME BACK HERE!
YEAH, LET'S GET THE EGG!
COME BACK SO I CAN EAT YOU!
BE EASIER TO CATCH THE DANG EGG IF SOMEBODY WOULD TURN ON THE LIGHTS!
?
?
A WALKING EGG!
WHY DON'T YOU WANT TO BE COOKED!?
AW MAN, THE KING'S GONNA LOVE THIS! SEIZE IT!

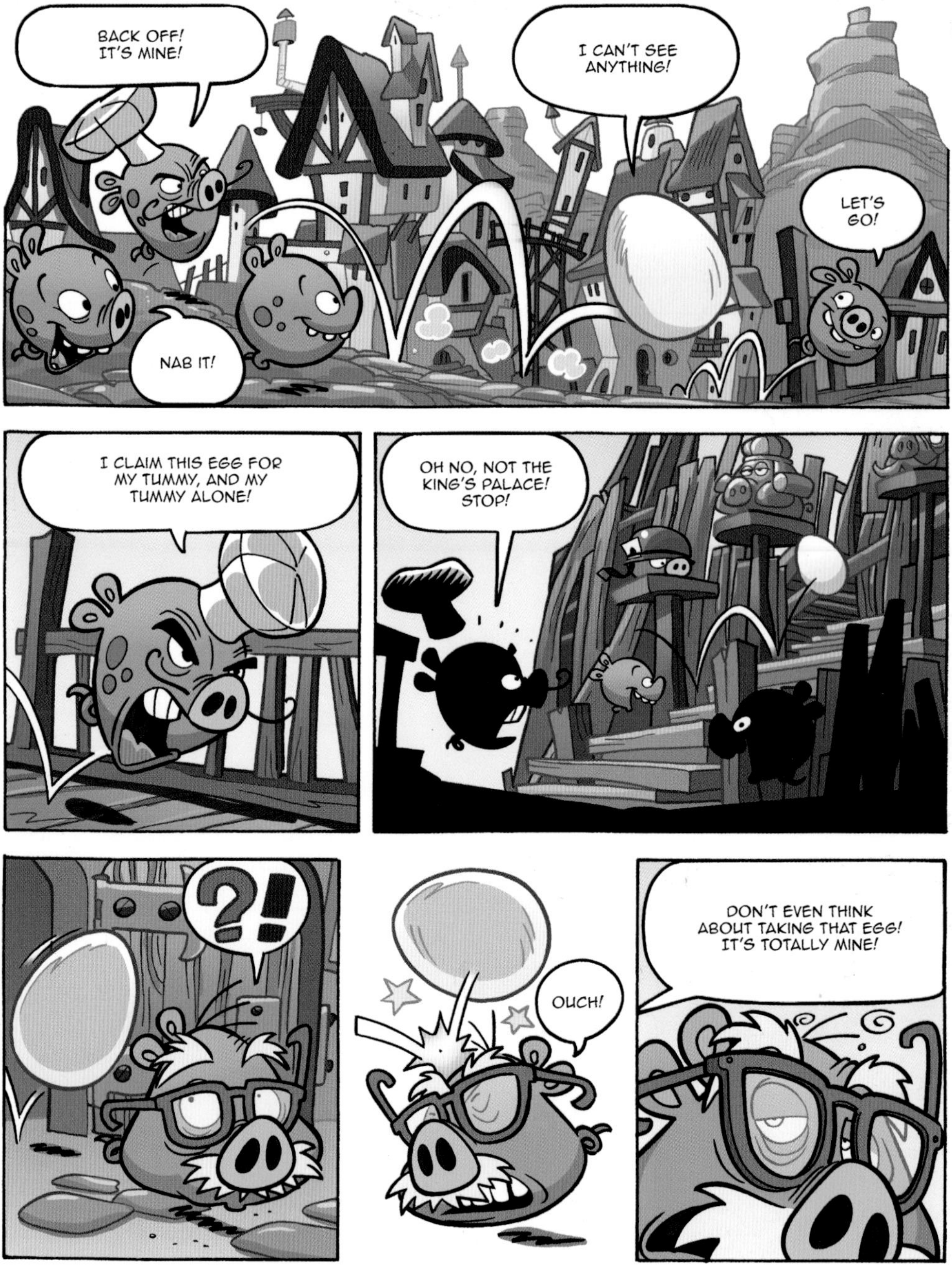
BACK OFF! IT'S MINE!
NAB IT!
I CAN'T SEE ANYTHING!
LET'S GO!
I CLAIM THIS EGG FOR MY TUMMY, AND MY TUMMY ALONE!
OH NO, NOT THE KING'S PALACE! STOP!
?!
OUCH!
DON'T EVEN THINK ABOUT TAKING THAT EGG! IT'S TOTALLY MINE!

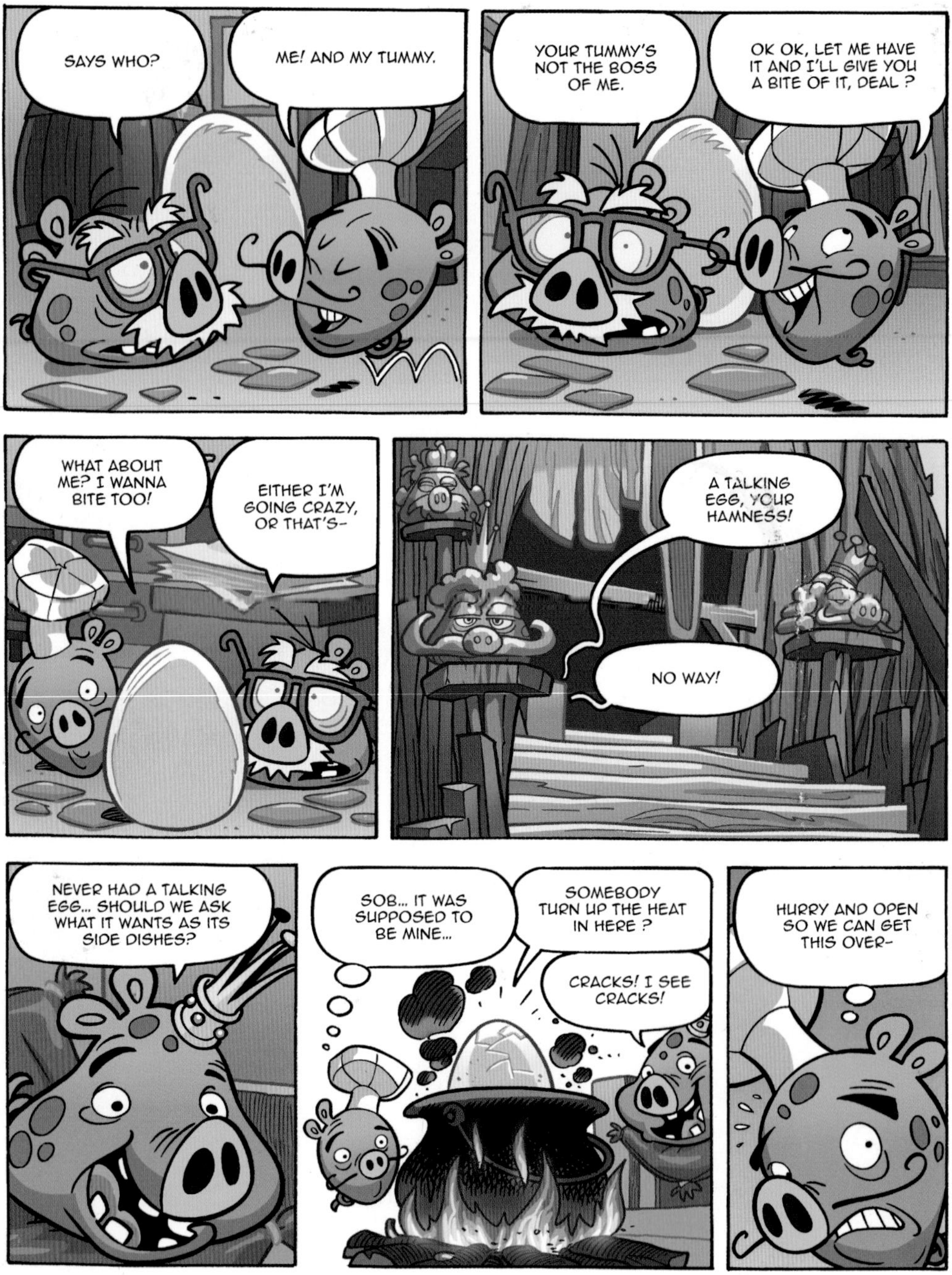
SAYS WHO?
ME! AND MY TUMMY.
YOUR TUMMY'S NOT THE BOSS OF ME.
OK OK, LET ME HAVE IT AND I'LL GIVE YOU A BITE OF IT, DEAL ?
WHAT ABOUT ME? I WANNA BITE TOO!
EITHER I'M GOING CRAZY, OR THAT'S-
A TALKING EGG, YOUR HAMNESS!
NO WAY!
NEVER HAD A TALKING EGG... SHOULD WE ASK WHAT IT WANTS AS ITS SIDE DISHES?
SOB... IT WAS SUPPOSED TO BE MINE...
SOMEBODY TURN UP THE HEAT IN HERE ?
CRACKS! I SEE CRACKS!
HURRY AND OPEN SO WE CAN GET THIS OVER-

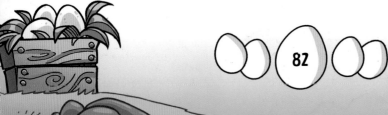

WHOA!
HOOOOOOOOOOOOO FEELIN' HOT!
THERE HE IS! WE'VE BEEN LOOKING FOR THAT GUY EVERYWHERE.
BUT, WHAT'S HE DOING IN AN EGG?
THAT'S NO EGG... JUST A PLASTER EGG-SHAPED MOLD WE MADE TO DECORATE THE PALACE.
THEY'RE REALLY HEAVY, SO WE BUILD THEM IN TWO PARTS THEN PUT THEM TOGETHER. HE MUST'VE FALLEN ASLEEP IN ONE OF THE PARTS...
Z
THIS ONE'S DONE!
GUESS WE'LL HAVE TO BUILD A NEW ONE...
BUHUHU... I CAN'T EAT PLASTER !
Y-YOU MEAN...
ALL THIS TROUBLE...
...FOR A PLASTERED PIG!!!!
THE END!

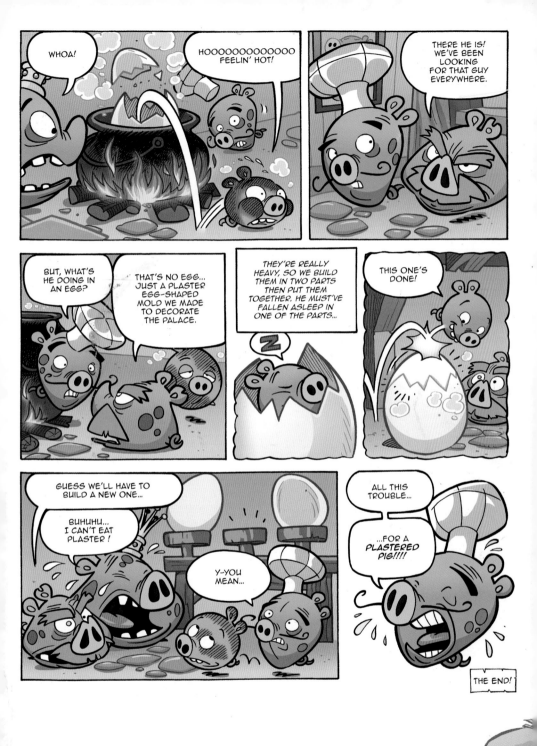

ANGRY BIRDS COMICS

ANGRY BIRDS COMICS: WELCOME TO THE FLOCK

ANGRY BIRDS COMICS: WHEN PIGS FLY

ANGRY BIRDS COMICS: SKY HIGH

ANGRY BIRDS COMICS: FLY OFF THE HANDLE

More *Angry Birds* collections from IDW Publishing.

Catch up on all of the adventures featuring Angry Birds, the world's most popular mobile game franchise. Each hardcover collection features your favorite Angry Birds characters in ways that you've never seen them before!

IDW ⤜ROVIO KAIKEN PUBLISHING LTD.

WWW.IDWPUBLISHING.COM